# CHANT OF DEATH

To Susanna,

Gracious thanks for
your review and

Much Love,
Diane

# Also by Diane Marquart Moore

**Non-Fiction**
Iran: In a Persian market *(1980)*
Their Adventurous Will: Profiles of Memorable Louisiana Women *(1984)*
Live Oak Gardens *(1991)*
Treasures of Avery Island *(2001)*

**Fiction**
Nothing for Free *(2008)*
The Maine Event *(2010)*

### Young Adult Fiction
Martin's Quest *(1995)*
Sophie's Sojourn in Persia *(2004)*
Kajun Kween *(2005)*
Flood on the Rio Teche *(2007)*
Martin Finds His Totem *(2008)*
Goat Man Murder *(2010)*

**Poetry**
Grandma's "Good War": A Verse Retrospective of the Forties *(2008)*
The Holy Present and Farda *(2009)*

### Poetry for Children
The Beast Beezlebufo *(2010)*


# Also by Isabel Anders

**Non-Fiction**
Awaiting the Child *(1987, 2005)*
The Faces of Friendship *(1992, 2008)*
Simple Blessings for Sacred Moments *(1998)*
Soul Moments: Times When Heaven Touches Earth *(2000, 2006)*
40-Day Journey with Madeleine L'Engle *(2009)*
Becoming Flame: Uncommon Mother-Daughter Wisdom *(2010)*

**For Children**
Sand and Shells, Carousels and Silver Bells: A Child's Seasons of Prayers *(1996)*
The Real Night Before Christmas *(1999)*
Easter ABCs *(2000)*

# Chant of Death

## A Father Malachi Mystery

## by Diane Marquart Moore & Isabel Anders

*We will fulfill this sacred number of seven if we satisfy our obligations of service at Lauds, Prime, Terce, Sext, None, Vespers and Compline, for it was of these hours during the day that he said: Seven times a day have I praised you.*

⁓The Rule of St. Benedict

Pinyon Publishing
Montrose, CO

First Edition: 2010

Pinyon Publishing
23847 V66 Trail, Montrose, CO 81403
www.pinyon-publishing.com

Library of Congress Control Number: 2010932659
ISBN: 978-0-9821561-7-9

for Vickie and Bill

# PROLOGUE

*...there are the monks called gyrovagues, who spend their entire lives drifting from region to region, staying as guests for three or four days in different monasteries. Always on the move, they never settle down, and are slaves to their own wills and gross appetites.*
*—Benedict, on* The Kinds of Monks *in* The Holy Rule of St. Benedict

November 30, St. Andrew's Day

Ed O'Hirlihy, keeping bar, had seen the large, disheveled, red-robed figure enter more than two hours earlier, with what looked like a katana, a Samurai sword, encased in a wooden saya, dangling from his rope belt.

A little late for Halloween! Ed thought. It was late November, and in the cool southern Louisiana evening the flamboyant monk wore no outer cloak.

Ed didn't think much of it at first. He'd heard that the old itinerant, Father Eli, was staying at the local St. Andrew's Abbey, though he had national prominence as a would-be 'prophet.' So what? Religious could drink, and Eli was rumored to have both Japanese and Russian blood. He was a real international lightning rod.

It was after the fifth round of beers, when the good Father was on his third Vodka straight, that things got dicey. Fr. Eli Jahrles, known to some as 'Eli-Jah' for his pretensions about being a prophet, had become agitated and was now standing unsteadily on a wooden bench at a table surrounded by other losers.

As Fr. Eli waved his tuniced arms and the sword swayed in its scabbard, Ed winced. He didn't want his establishment going to the dogs in one evening.

Suddenly Fr. Eli jumped down, dramatically marched to a

1

central spot in front of the row of stools at the bar, and shouted out an unrecognizable epithet that got the attention of even the drowsiest drunks in the place. He deftly pulled the slender, two-and-a-half-foot sword from its sheath, careful not to slice his own huge callused hands, and with its tip drew a circle around himself on the rough floor.

Then Fr. Eli-Jah began performing what looked like a carefully choreographed dance, enhanced with Cossack movements. For an old fart, he was surprisingly light on his feet. But it was the mask-like solemnity on his rugged face, and then, when he had finished, his guttural outcry, that made nearly everyone in The Camellia Bar suddenly freeze to attention:

*"Vengeance is mine...!"* The startled reactions of the drinkers that broke out served to muffle the rest of his pronouncement. Who was this kook, anyway?

Ed, who had been taught well by the nuns but who considered himself a burnt-out case, knew the quote. *"Says the Lord,"* he muttered to himself, before stepping in to settle the unease that had taken over the atmosphere in his pub.

But before Ed could manage to lead the disruptive figure toward his swinging exit doors, the old monk managed to swipe at the rough oak pillars and put a long gouge in one.

Imagining worse outcomes, Ed the atheist breathed a prayer of thanks that it had only scratched wood.

Why couldn't the Abbey keep its guests better ensconced and out of the community's hair? The bar owner sighed and turned back to the business of wiping down the bar.

# CHAPTER 1

*Unity is the principle of all things and the most dominant of all that is: all things emanate from it and it emanates from nothing.*

~Theon of Smyrna

As soon as Father Malachi opened the door from the sacristy and entered the chapel, he sensed sacrilege before he actually saw the wet pile of blackened wood ashes in the center of the altar. He was as shocked as he would have been had he come upon a cremated Jesus heaped in a mound on the fair linen cloth. The scent of burned wood overpowered the usual scent of candle wax and the astringent incense he had used at High Mass the day before. Who could have desecrated their sacred space in this manner?

Father Malachi differed from his fellow monks in that he had married and lived in the world before he became a seminarian, then a monk, and, now, an abbot. As a healer, he knew the limitations of wounded human beings for his own wife had committed suicide years ago. But he was still sickened at the sight of some warped creature's idea of creativity. A note lay beside the charred mess, and after closer inspection, Fr. Malachi saw that the pile contained the remnants of burnt religious cards, some bearing the image of Jesus. The note, written in poorly formed letters, read: *Yore not gods.*

He couldn't help thinking: Hell has terrible grammar. And lousy decorum. Someone had been setting up an 'alternative' display on the altar, had burned holy symbols and heaped the offensive ash on the corporal during the night. Who had done this? One of the monks at his beloved St. Andrew's Abbey? Not possible. One of the secular helpers or suppliers in their bread baking operation? Possibly. Maybe the shabby, sullen 'handyman' who had come seeking work recently? He knew the sacristy had been locked the night before, as always, keeping the sacred vessels safe. How had the person gained entrance in order to take the cards and do this?

Father Malachi glanced up at the statue of the Virgin Mary in her immaculate blue gown, standing on a snake that had its red fangs extended. "Blessed among women, and blessed be the fruit of your womb," he said, taking the corporal and folding it over respectfully to enclose the ash.

He crossed himself before a wooden replica of the crucified Christ hanging behind the altar and went about dressing it again, realizing it was 6:45 a.m., almost time for early Mass. No moments for meditation or investigation of the sacrilege. No ashy fingerprints visible. Malachi, whose genuine piety was matched by his unflappable logic, wondered why, in real life, the demands of existence always involved excruciating choices of what to give prime attention to.

In the sacristy, he put on his chasuble and purple stole and scratched his smoothly shaved head in perplexity. During his preparations, the Abbot's ring, a mounted gold medallion, suddenly caught the morning light, and his mind, as though in sync, exploded in outrage. Here it was Advent, the time of waiting for the Christ, and some twisted soul had tried to turn Him into ash before He materialized! The foolish menace didn't even have his seasons straight. "You're not gods" or "You're not God's"? It could be taken to have several meanings. Though the perp had fumbled the expression, the threat was clear enough.

Fr. Malachi, who had seen much worse in his career, still felt a strong prescience of evil lurking within the stone walls of the sacred residence. He heard the monks processing in, two by two, practicing their unembellished plainchants that usually transported him into contemplative realms. But he didn't experience his daily uplift.

The traditional mental picture of Gregory the Great receiving chants from the Holy Spirit with a dove sitting on his shoulder caused him to smile. Gregory had been a compiler, and there weren't any doves sitting on the shoulders of those who altered the Divine Harmonies in their efforts at post-modern commercialization, he thought ruefully. This had become the stickiest issue on his current slate as Abbot, and he really WAS going to have to make a decision about it soon.

The purity of chant composition had always been respected in the Benedictine monastic tradition. Devoted monks had acknowledged that the seven notes of the musical scale were sacred, just as the story of beginnings in Genesis told of *seven* days of creation. The octave, which consisted of seven notes in succession with a 'do' repeated an octave higher at the end, symbolized a coming together of Divine and earthly forces in a mellifluous flow of creative strength. Some even believed it was key to altering the level of vibration in the air, and when properly sung, heightened peacefulness in the community.

The practice of chant, for the monks, was not only an act of worship, it was a spiritual exercise, a creation of unity that the singers themselves brought into being. Even the novices understood that the perpetuation of the traditional tones in sequence were a powerful sign to the world that *God's order prevails in the universe,* that the Divine unity underlies all.

Was the sacrilege on the altar a crudely expressed message intended to chide the monks about crossing into the forbidden realm of the secular world, profaning ethereal music by making CDs of their plainchants and marketing them? Whose buttons had been pushed worst by the sudden change in the Abbey's material fortunes? The list of potential grievance bearers was too long for Malachi to contemplate now.

He had given the brothers permission to record the voices of The Heavenly Choir, as they called themselves. But, by doing so, had he invoked some kind of dark reprimand? As Abbot, father of the community and virtually their Christ, Fr. Malachi thought of his monks with paternal anxiety. As their leader, teacher, and ruler, it was his responsibility to investigate the desecration and find the Religious who had violated the peace of the Community; that is, if one of the monks had anything to do with the sacrilege. And this music venture they had launched might have to be scrapped, despite the wealth it brought.

He loved his flock, this community that was tangible evidence of his genuine midlife calling, and he wanted them to be happy in their lives at the Abbey. He also desired for them to have the proper disposition of heart. The chants helped them with that disposition, but he didn't want any obsession with them to cause the monks to replace the teachings of the Gospel, the centrality of the Word, or usurp their order's essential Benedictine Rule either, for that matter.

He felt that his wife, who had some years ago sought a kind of liberation from her demons by committing suicide with a handgun, would have benefited from The Rule.

The Rule of St. Benedict, founder of their order, was the true way of life, not a set of laws. Unfortunately, Fr. Malachi's wife had been extremely narcissistic, and God hadn't been the true point of reference in her life. The center of her circumference had been herself. She had possessed no stability, no conversion, no sense of otherness, and no listening powers. With those lacks, it was a wonder she had survived to the age of 30.

In his previous work as a psychiatrist dealing with disordered minds, Fr. Malachi had revered Jung; but he found that St. Benedict knew more about the human psyche than Jung. The legendary saint had a grasp of this thing called *unity* that had been perverted by dualistic religions. After his wife died, Fr. Malachi found a way of returning to his heart through reading about the Rule of St. Benedict that had been written in vernacular Latin during the 6th century. Nine thousand words had changed his life.

Fr. Malachi sighed and thought about the chants again. He wasn't a musician himself, and the sequences had been difficult for him to learn. He respected the talent of his young cantor and choirmaster, Fr. Paul, who had a sublime voice, and felt he could trust Fr. Paul's skills and intense commitment to making the chants a success. However, he also knew that some monasteries were allowing their chants to be characterized as musical preparation for the Apocalypse, which was a bow to the fundamentalists in order to sell more copies.

Malachi relied on the supreme importance of love in the biblical book of First John to guide him, and he knew that he could achieve that love only through humility. He sighed again, remembering his previous days of work with people who were mentally disturbed. Their willfulness had made him cynical, which, in turn, made humility even more difficult, but...

Fr. Malachi returned to his thoughts about loving his flock and wanting them to be happy. Yet, he also realized the necessity of tough love. On a bulletin beside the sacristy sink, Fr. Malachi had only yesterday posted these words from St. Benedict: "If there are artisans in the monastery, they are to practice their craft with all humility, but only with the abbot's permission. If one of them becomes puffed up by his skillfulness in his craft and feels that he is conferring something on the monastery, he is to be removed from practicing his craft and not allowed to resume it unless, after manifesting his humility, he is so ordered by the abbot..." Fr. Malachi had also enjoined his fellow monks to read this rule at Noonday Prayer and to commit it to memory.

He thought that the baking of bread by the Order to sell at the Farmer's Market in Marksville every Friday was a worthwhile enterprise, although the proceeds had been modest, compared to the staggering profits already garnered from the CD sales. The stalwart Fr. Frank had been in charge of bread production for many years, and relying on his expert administration of the process, Malachi had hardly needed to supervise. It all worked like clockwork. Part of the proceeds was dispersed to at least ten charities in the area, just enough donations to keep the monastery from appearing to be a commercial operation. The Diocese provided some upkeep for their Order, but they had supported themselves well enough through their own baking and gardening skills for the better part of 100 years.

The sound of bells startled his reverie and summoned him once again to his sacred purpose. He glanced out the sacristy window at the line of monks in their white tunics, hands inside apron-like black scapulars, processing along the trellised walkway to the chapel, two by two, subdued by their own chanting. No time to ponder the ashy mess in the sacristy sink, but the monks wouldn't escape his interrogation before breakfast. He'd call a meeting in the library while they were still fasting.

Fr. Malachi walked out to the altar to begin the service, genuflected before it, and went over to stand beside his chair, allowing himself to be transported by the clear voices of the now assembled monks as they began to chant the Introit.

Some invisible prod caused him to look up. The painted angels swirling in a circle on the ceiling above his head suddenly begged his attention, as though they had added their voices in song, and he was caught up in peripheral awareness that something else had gone very wrong this morning. He stared, dumbfounded, at a gaping hole in the once-pink face of one of the cherubs that had been artfully rendered by the famous Dutch artist, Jon Vroon. The faceless cherub now looked like a Martian creature who had invaded the ring of winged messengers. Amid the soaring voices of The Heavenly Choir, Fr. Malachi drew back as though he had been punched in the face.

"Holy Bleedin' Zerubbabel!" The words spurted out of his mouth in spite of himself.

# CHAPTER II

*Music paints the reality in darker colors by increasing the sorrow of the sorrowful and the happiness of the happy.*
— **Arab proverb**

Fr. Paul, lead cantor and choirmaster, so often absorbed in the sound of his own matchless tenor voice, noticed the startled expression on the Abbot's face and the burst of a strange exclamation coming from his mouth, interrupting the Introit. But he couldn't make out what the Abbot had inappropriately interjected during the antiphonal chant.

He scrutinized the Abbot's face while he sang, anticipating his big solo moments during responsorial psalms. Sometimes he accorded himself the privilege of being the soloist at the close of the service when he intoned the *Salve, Regina*. However, Fr. Paul didn't possess the restraint and piety typical of cantors during the Middle Ages. Instead, he was a born performer, and with the unprecedented success of the monks' latest album, he now regarded himself as a notable, cutting-edge contemporary artist. Recently one young female admirer had even told him he resembled the rock singer Sting, he thought fondly to himself.

As the service moved into the Offertory, Fr. Paul noticed that the Abbot's hands trembled when he raised the chalice. What was wrong with him today? Maybe Fr. Malachi was overworked, even burned out, and couldn't really handle the work of publicizing the CDs for The Heavenly Choir. As the cantor, Fr. Paul himself had offered to be the designated emissary of the choir, taking their gifts of prayerful, poignant chant to the world, and the Abbot hadn't let him. Even so, Fr. Paul eagerly anticipated an upcoming interview the Abbot had arranged with a New Orleans television station. Fr. Paul smiled widely during a response, and the Abbot acknowledged it with a significant frown. No ambiguity there. This was going to be a power struggle.

As the Recessional began, Fr. Paul observed that the Abbot seemed about to speak, then motioned for the monks to proceed. At the door of the chapel, the Abbot met them and held up a hand. "Breakfast will be a little late this morning," he announced brusquely. "I've instructed the cooks to join you in my private library, and I hope we'll have a brief meeting about an incident... " He stopped and corrected himself. "About TWO irregularities that have occurred in the sanctuary." It took inner discipline to hold back his emotion. "I'll meet you there – now," he emphasized. "No lollygagging, please."

Fr. Malachi's peremptory tone surprised Fr. Paul. Fr. Malachi, over six feet tall, was an imposing figure of authority, but he was usually a man of equable temperament.

Fr. Paul, himself head and shoulders above most of the brothers, followed the other monks down the stone-arched walkway leading to the administrative offices, his stomach growling angrily at what seemed an unnecessary interruption of his meal routine.

To distract himself, he hummed a forceful, angular rock adaptation of the Gregorian chants popularized by the Deathspell Omega band, whose leader had actually written to him! Fr. Paul was not averse to these popularized riffs on ancient plainchant. Imitation, to him, was the greatest compliment and only indicated how famous Paul, and the others, had now become.

As the monks walked, two abreast, up the stark hall of the administration building toward the Abbot's library, they paused to skirt the monastery's ever-present housemaid Cotille, who was on her knees waxing the marble floors. Cotille, a wiry woman of indeterminate age, had the typical olive-hued skin of a Louisiana Cajun. She cleaned the monastery and chapel with the ferocity characteristic of most Cajun women, who kept their homes scrupulously maintained. Based on the fusty smell that usually permeated the hall, her battle with mold and mildew seemed endless.

She wore a long-sleeved, flawlessly laundered cotton blouse year-round, and her arms flew in deft movements as she applied paste wax to large squares of the footworn gray and white marble. She looked up at the cantor with her tense black eyes and down again without speaking. Fr. Paul considered her flat affect a sign of mild retardation, and thought he was being solicitous of her because of this handicap. But she ignored his condescension, mumbling a few archaic French words that reflected her ancestry, that of the Acadians who had been exiled from Nova Scotia in the 18th century.

Cotille shared three meals daily with the monks and sat unsmiling, eating ravenously as if she spent no money on groceries at home. No one knew where she lodged, and, unfortunately, no one cared. Once she had gone to the Abbot for Confession, and as far as Fr. Paul could discern, she had never repeated the act, even though she attended Mass on Sundays and often joined the monks for Evensong.

Cotille was a woman who seemed never to have birthed anything. Some of the monks believed that she had been molested by a priest in her church in St. John the Baptist Parish, but no one knew the circumstances. She was superstitious and frequently appeared with a knotted string around her neck, evidence of a belief in *traiteurs,* the Cajun healers who boasted they cured those who suffered from rheumatism by wearing such strings.

Fr. Paul tried, but couldn't hide his disdain for the wretched woman. Yet she remained devoted to all the monks at St. Andrew's, who wondered what the Abbot had said to her that she refused to return to the confessional stall. Paul glanced back at the woman and met her continually blinking eyes. Something about the stricken look on her normally impassive face caused Fr. Paul to feel uncomfortable. He bumped into the two monks walking ahead of him.

☙

In the dimly lit library where four highly polished oak tables had been pushed together, the monks sat, complaining about the delay of breakfast. The half-dark room also held a maroon leather sofa, its back cushions deeply indented, giving the impression that the Abbot had received many visitors seeking counsel during his short tenure. He was a highly accessible priest and trustworthy confidant who welcomed all, often commenting, though he didn't remember the source, "Nothing human is alien to me."

Lining the walls of the room were tall oak bookshelves filled with 'tomes,' as the Abbot called them, the cumbersome titles, often in Latin, confronting the monks who seldom read anything except Scripture and their breviaries anymore. However, the Abbot didn't pressure his monks into theological discourse, preferring a faith supported by the Benedictine Rule, which was just a matter of *inner and outer order,* he emphasized.

The one large picture window in the room looked out on a courtyard, the centerpiece of which was a small pool lined by tall, sprightly daylilies. A pair of white mandarin geese preened energetically at the pool's edge. Beyond the pool, a large lake rippled in the distance. The northern wind suddenly gusted, announcing a ubiquitous Louisiana thunderstorm, and lush Spanish moss on the old oak shadowing the pool trailed in the wind, some gray tendrils of the moss loosening and falling on the rye grass the monks had planted for winter color. Storms inside and out, the Abbot thought.

He stood in the center of the room, his stern expression causing the other monks to feel uneasy, shuffling his heavy feet in the ankle-high leather shoes that seemed so incongruous poking out from under his alb.

"When I entered the chapel before Mass this morning, I found a mound of ashes heaped on the linen cloth in the center of the altar," he began calmly. He hurried on with his story before he could be questioned. "And beside it was a threatening message no doubt intended as a reprimand toward us for recording CDs of our chants and marketing them." The Abbot said the words flatly and paused. The room became noisy with whispers.

Fr. Malachi held up a hand. "You can read the note later. As if this were not enough sacrilege during Mass, I observed that the entire face of one of the cherubs painted on the ceiling of the chapel has been cut away. I checked the floor underneath afterward, but the vandal had obviously swept up, and there were only small specks of dried paint left from the scraping." He didn't mention the bits of religious cards in the ashes; perhaps their provenance could be traced later.

The monks looked at one another like schoolboys accused of stealing classroom property. Fr. Jean, the Abbot's assistant, regarded the Abbot with troubled dark eyes. His handsome face of a soft butterscotch color stood out among the others. Fr. Jean had come over from Haiti to join the Benedictines at St. Andrew's only a few years after the Abbot had taken over as leader of the community. He had been made Prior almost immediately, and he deeply revered his superior.

Fr. Jean was so connected in spirit to the Abbot that he felt every nuance of upset the older priest experienced. Fr. Jean shook his head back and forth in consternation. He had seen voodoo, Santeria, and superstition muddy the religious climate of his native country and knew that despite what one thought of the 'power' behind these practices, lives were often lost in those circles. The desecration of the altar was to Fr. Jean as serious as an omen or a curse, a precursor of some kind of perverse magic or evildoing.

"We're shocked at these defilements," Fr. Jean said slowly, striving for precise speech. "Surely none of us would commit such an act." He searched the faces of the other monks huddled at the table, and they looked at one another, wondering if indeed one of them had turned traitor. Doubt and suspicion began to permeate the holy calm that most of the monks had assumed along with the communal air they breathed.

"Whoever did this is severely wounded spiritually," Fr. Jean said softly, but clearly audibly. "I suggest that we continue our fast and return to prayer."

The monks began murmuring and grousing and started looking around accusingly at one another. This was the worst thing that could happen among them—the planting of seeds of dissension and an erosion of trust. The Abbot, whose hunger had by now become an irritant, and who had been anticipating a platter of eggs, biscuits, and sausage, bristled. No one cared more about truth, beauty, and restoring blessed equanimity. But not on an empty stomach.

"Ah, Fr. Jean, you're always about doing penance for mankind," the Abbot chided his noble second-in-command gently. "But I don't want to see us turning on one another because of these incidents, and your idea about depriving ourselves seems to be inviting a disruption in community order. Perhaps a hearty breakfast will help us think better. Surely someone from the 'outside' has entered and attacked our sanctuary. I don't think anyone among the brothers would ever commit such sacrilege, and enforced piety isn't going to solve this." The Abbot gave his conscientious monk a concise smile and was about to dismiss his flock when the door to the library opened widely, banging the wall behind it.

Cotille stood in the doorframe, waving the blackened, soiled linen she had just found in the sacristy sink. She appeared more stricken than usual. "Who wrapped those ashes in the holy linen cloth?" she demanded, uncharacteristically, of the startled monks.

Hearing the unusual tone of ferocity in her voice, the monks began buzzing among themselves. *Who, indeed?*

# CHAPTER III

*The companions of right reason are decency, cadence, and accord; decency in song, accord in harmony, cadence in rhythm.*

*≈* **Plato**

*"Let us now praise famous men..."*

The underlying murmur of trained male voices was an ever-present fact of monastic life. This morning, a small group of monks who had taken to heart Fr. Jean's counsel to continue fasting had gone back to the chapel to practice the familiar hymn.

Fr. Eli Jahrles, making his way, cane prod by cane prod, down the cobbled path to the refectory, was, as always, late for breakfast. Sometime guest at St. Andrew's, wanted or not, he still wasn't about to miss a free meal.

Despite the rumbling of his stomach, he couldn't help paying attention to the hymn based on the words of the wisdom writer Sirach, that had broken into his reverie. It continued: *"...The Lord apportioned to them great glory..."*

"Ha! Glory or infamy? The mockery of this place and its acolytes will come to a bitter end," he muttered to himself. *"Sic transit Gloria mundi."*

He was among the brothers but not *of* them in his contrarian position as a frequent occupant of the monks' one-room guest cottage behind the garden. Fr. Eli was neither an official inquisitor from the Church hierarchy nor an elder patriarch of benign presence, and the ambiguity of his position served to keep most of the monks slightly unsettled.

"The Abbot shouldn't put up with him," Fr. Paul had noted on more than one occasion. "He should run the old tramp out on general principles."

Eli-Jah, as the press had facetiously dubbed 'the prophet,' seemed ubiquitous these days. His incendiary presence and

15

outbursts on more than one occasion of clergy gatherings had been noted and written up in *The St. Helena Times* and even picked up on by the AP.

Fr. Eli could always be counted on as a barometer and censor of events that seemed to attribute more glory to men than to God, and he wasn't one to mince his Latin in response.

"...Their posterity will continue forever, and their glory will not be blotted out," the perfectly sung á cappella lines of the hymn continued to float out into the crisp fall air. "Ah, and does Fr. Paul think to mitigate the damage his crass creations have wrought by interspersing his sacrilege with hymns and true spiritual songs?" Fr. Eli spoke aloud and spat loudly into the nearest fenced garden plot. A white-robed figure, who couldn't avoid passing him on the path, pulled away and nearly stumbled.

More than one of the younger monks had felt spooked by the probing stare of the unkempt prophet who lurked in the corridors and sometimes brandished a knife resembling a small sword at dinner as though it were designed to pierce bone and marrow. The beefy head cook shuddered and crossed herself when filling Fr. Eli's bowl with her soup of monastery-grown vegetables and when she set out plates of brown bread on the rough-hewn tables. Despite the dimensions of her ample frame, she was careful not to come too close to him and envisioned him tripping her with his unwieldy, knotted cane.

As Fr. Eli approached the refectory, the aroma of freshly ground coffee and the pungent scent of skillet grease led him into the dining area. The refectory was a cavernous room, its largeness made warmer by two brilliantly hued murals painted on the walls at each end of the room: one of the Last Supper, and another of the Angel Gabriel's Annunciation to the Virgin Mary. Both had been rendered by Jon Vroon, the Dutch artist who had spent several years transforming the common rooms and chapel of the Abbey into unique treasures.

"They may sing like angels, but every angel brings terror," Fr. Eli muttered to himself, quoting the poet Rilke as he joined the line of monks whose plates were being filled at the food warming station. After he had loudly, and with wide gestures, instructed the cook to serve him a generous serving of eggs and sausage and filled his own mug with coffee, he hobbled over to an unoccupied table in the back of the refectory where he sat down, glaring at any monk who appeared to be approaching his table.

Fr. Eli slurped his coffee loudly, ignoring the monks who overheard the noise and frowned at him. The white alb draped on his ungainly form had a design of coffee stains that formed concentric circles on its high-buttoned top. At least today he had conformed to the standard of common white, but he had omitted the scapular. He sometimes inexplicably appeared among them in an ancient tattered red alb, looking more like an overgrown choirboy or a Victorian judge minus the wig. The visual dissonance of red among white had led someone to dub him "the devil among the sheep." But the difference seemed to lend him a quirky, elevated status in which he reveled.

Today, as always, his gray, curly beard seemed matted with neglect or the remnants of old meals. Fr. Eli's distracting unkemptness clearly repulsed most of the monks, except for the Abbot and Fr. Jean.

Fr. Malachi approached and put down his platter on Eli's table, pulling out a chair across from the eccentric figure so that he could study his face. The Abbot knew that the old man would not refuse him a seat at his table. Although Fr. Eli abused the Abbey's hospitality with his loud denouncements of the life and practices of the monastery, he dared not challenge the authority of the father superior of St. Andrew's, as his bed and board depended on the charity of the Abbot.

"Why weren't you at Mass, Father?" the Abbot asked neutrally.

"I was receiving realizations, revelations, and realities that common souls know nothing of," Fr. Eli replied.

"Revelations, realizations, realities?"

Fr. Eli scratched his long hawkish nose and withdrew a folded paper from the pocket of his stained tunic. "Yes, such darkness gathers around me, but annunciations have come through the angels. They are messengers of the archetypes. I hear and feel their energy. What has happened to common decency? Do you not know that the Unity is in peril in this place?"

Fr. Eli pulled on one enormous ear and smote his own chest three times. He glanced at the depiction of the Angel Gabriel at the far end of the room, pointed at it, and intoned as though he spoke mainly for his own benefit. "Origen was right! All the air is filled with angels. They announce grace in spite of these sons of abomination who in our very presence are making a mockery of the unity and purity of the octave! If they aren't stopped they will return us all to the primordial chaos!"

Fr. Eli skewered a piece of pork sausage with his fork, thrust it into his mouth, and chewed it vigorously. He put his head down, and held a hand up vertically, palm forward, signaling he wanted no reply.

He's so much like some of my former patients, the Abbot thought. He surmised that when Fr. Eli spoke of mockery he was referring to the unorthodox addition of instruments to the chant when they recorded at the studio and to Fr. Paul's subtle, creative alterations of the traditional plainchant melodies. He ignored the monk's unwillingness to explain further and asked, "What will you do with your revelations, realizations, and realities?"

"I've begun distributing copies of them to the world." Fr. Eli sopped his plate with a biscuit and slurped more coffee. "It is my duty, and my holy calling in this life. Even though I stand alone."

The Abbot was alarmed. Papers distributed? The note on the altar? No, if Fr. Eli had composed it, it would have been in harsh but flawless Latin. Then who?

Fr. Eli, suddenly enlivened, explained as though to a child: "Angels respond to singing, you know. When we sing, we're granted wisdom and can understand things not known before. It's in the *Zohar*. But if you sully the song lines when they're supposed to emanate from the soul, unadorned by instrument, you call up dark angels. We're supposed to sing radiantly." Fr. Eli stood and pushed back his chair. "Your fearful destiny is determined by the very music you make!" He spat out the words so that they sounded less like traditional monastic wisdom and more like a personal threat.

The Abbot watched the figure he had begun to perceive was paranoid schizophrenic in a delusional state walk out of the refectory, counting something on his own outspread fingers and mumbling his revelations, realizations, and realities—perhaps to the angels.

℞

Outdoors, the rain had abated, and a faint sun appeared above the bell tower atop the chapel. Fr. Eli paced the trellised meditation walk, head bowed as if in prayer and shivering in the brisk November wind. He heard the hum of a motor, and a short white van with NOPB-TV painted on its side came into view. A cameraman boasting a fulsome beard and hair to his shoulders, and a young woman, hair standing up in red spikes, got out of the van and approached him.

"Where can we find Fr. Paul?" the young woman asked. She peered at him closely. "You're Fr. Eli-Jah!" she exclaimed.

"*Quem Quaeritis.* Whom are you seeking?" Fr. Eli smiled thinly. "Yes, you need not explain. I am the one you seek."

"Well, we were really..." Her words trailed off as she appraised the disheveled monk standing before her. Visibly excited, she motioned the cameraman to come closer.

"You're the visionary everyone is talking about. If you'll give me a few moments, I'll just jot down some ideas and questions, and we'll record an interview. I'm Sarah and this is Bill, my cameraman." The long-haired man smiled at Fr. Eli and was rewarded with a grunt from the monk.

"I make documentaries for the station," Sarah said. She regarded Fr. Eli with clear blue eyes. "Do you mind waiting a few minutes, Father?" She seemed unsure how to address the strange figure.

"I can wait," Fr. Eli replied, uncharacteristically biddable. "I'll sit down and work on my writings." He pulled out the paper from his pocket again and sat down on a small stone bench at the side of the walkway, defying the breeze to blow his work away. Bill and Sarah huddled on the walk and began moving their hands in the air and whispering with one another.

"Let the interrogation begin," Fr. Eli demanded aloud. He jotted something on the paper, read it, folded it again, then repeated the motion several times, finally slipping it back into the pocket of his alb. His face was clenched in the manner of a man prepared to defend his own life and purpose to the death.

Sarah and Bill approached. Bill unbuttoned Fr. Eli's alb and clipped a small microphone to it. He stepped away from the agitated figure hastily.

"I need to record approximately five minutes of background for our interview," Sarah explained calmly. "When I finish, Bill will tell you how to sit and where to look to get the best shots of your face."

Fr. Eli sat erect, as though waiting to be shot, smiling grimly through clenched teeth. Sarah moistened her lips, smoothed the spiked hair with one hand, and began speaking.

"This is Sarah Hines, bringing you a live interview with Fr. Eli Jahrles, here on the grounds of St. Andrew's Monastery. Fr. Eli is popularly known as Eli-Jah (as some have contracted his two names) and has reportedly been heard to imply that he himself fulfills this prophetic role on the world stage. Claiming to be the former Father Superior of an unnamed Eastern European order, Jahrles apparently views himself as an emissary or modern equivalent of that renowned prophet of Old Testament fame, also said to have appeared with Jesus on the Mount of Transfiguration in the Gospels. Elijah, who, according to the first book of Kings in the Bible, did not die but was taken to heaven in a chariot of fire, is important as a figure of hope and deliverance to both Christians and Jews.

"When Jewish families today enact the rite of the Seder, which celebrates their liberation from Egypt thousands of years ago, they will typically include an empty chair and place setting for the prophet Elijah to 'drop in.' Legend has it that Elijah comes unseen, and children look for a few drops missing from his wine cup, to prove he has been among them.

"Both Jesus and John the Baptist were thought of by some contemporaries as the 'New Elijah,' or a return of the long-dead prophet, come to liberate the Jews from the Romans."

Sarah paused briefly to allow for dramatic effect. "It is unclear exactly how Fr. Eli-Jah views his own role in this ancient prophetic line, but the return of the prophet Elijah is often connected with performing the final miracle before the coming of the Messiah, something even his followers admit that Fr. Eli has yet to accomplish. It is predicted that the true Elijah will 'reconcile the hearts of fathers to sons and the hearts of sons to fathers.' But this prophet Eli-Jah seems more of a divisive figure in his recent public comments concerning the unprecedented success of The Heavenly Choir, as they call themselves, at St. Andrew's Abbey. The choir's wildly popular recording of Gregorian Chants, *Godspeak*, recently hit Gold on the charts..."

As Sarah articulated the long introduction, Fr. Eli sat

impassively, reacting visibly only when she had interjected words such as 'reportedly,' 'claiming to,' and 'divisive.' When she had finished, he stood abruptly, awkwardly stabbing his cane in the ground for support, but Bill motioned for him to sit down and look directly at the cameraman.

Sarah plunged into the interview. "Fr. Eli, exactly what is it about the monks' success that you seem to feel profanes the tradition?"

Fr. Eli made a strange gargling noise in his throat before he began speaking. "Is there no end to the sacrilege? They seek to harness for their own ends what is a Holy Inheritance of the Lord! Our Lord himself cried out, 'They know not what they do!' What rough beast now 'slouches toward Bethlehem' to be born? Ah, but all is not lost. 'And he shall purify the sons of Levi.'" Fr. Eli threw up his huge hands in despair as if his audience wouldn't understand his message.

Undaunted, Sarah asked, "Is it the modern adaptations of the chants for which Fr. Paul is so famous that you find are such a violation, or the commercial success of both the ancient and the modern chant recordings?"

Fr. Eli began speaking in a chant-like voice, "'Hear, O Israel, the Lord our God, the Lord is one.' They profane the oneness, they deny the Holy One. In the morning they will cry, 'Would to God it were night,' and in the night watch they shall lament, 'Would to God it were day,' and the anger of the Righteous One shall pervade even their secret chamber, until all is made right!"

Sarah recoiled from the strange incantation and asked, "Are you saying that the monks are in danger from within or from some element outside the community?"

Fr. Eli said simply, "Let those who have ears hear."

Sarah looked at the cameraman and signaled to him that the end of the interview was imminent. She shot a final question at the larger-than-life monk.

"Is it true that you see yourself as a key figure in whatever is unfolding through these events? You have been heard to claim that you yourself will occupy the chair of Elijah the prophet..."

Fr. Eli reared up, eyes blazing, flailing his arms, and screamed at the lens as though the camera itself were the enemy: "God will not be mocked. I say to you what I say to all: Beware! You have seen with your own eyes the beginning of the great unraveling, the final undoing!"

# CHAPTER IV

*Music is part of us, and either ennobles or degrades our behavior.*

≈ **Boethius**

**W**hat a lot of ruckus to begin the day, thought Fr. Malachi, especially coming off the Great Silence that the monks observed after finishing the evening Compline, until the end of the morning's Lauds.

The Abbot was kneeling in his cell, trying to pray. How can we be expected to maintain the proper balance of monastic life, as prescribed by St. Benedict, the Abbot mused: '*Cruce, libro, et atro,*' or 'Cross, book, and plow,' with adequate time devoted each day to prayer, study, and physical work? All of the agitation in the community was evidence that more silent time was needed for individuals to look within themselves, seek forgiveness, and refocus their lives on God. As a professional mind healer, the Abbot doubly valued the cure of silence and the practice of centering prayer. To Malachi, overcoming inner and outer chaos depended on complete surrender to the Lord of Order. He sighed to himself.

He was disturbed by the intrusion of the media once again on the dedicated world of the Abbey, but he had realized that once the *Godspeak* album was released and distributed, people would be curious about the monks and their daily lives. But why did they have to pounce on the most controversial figure within fifty miles who happened to be among them now — Fr. Eli? (He couldn't help stumbling over phrases such as 'the fly in the ointment' and 'the dog in the manger' when thinking of the old gadfly.)

But what if there *was* something to Eli-Jah's rantings, beyond the headline appeal and interpersonal buzz that an enigmatic figure could spark, especially in such an insular environment?

The Abbot remembered the novelist Flannery O'Connor's statement "To the almost deaf, you have to shout, and to the almost

22

blind, you have to paint in very large letters." That was the secular culture, all right. When the message was too subtle, they just didn't get it. But when someone larger than life like Fr. Eli appeared in public, loose arms flailing like windmills, people noticed. And there was no doubt that dis-ease *was* spreading, centered around the old nut. Yet, the mandate to hospitality kept him from banishing the prophet from their midst.

And Fr. Eli's warnings about the disintegration of unity in the Abbey, couched as they were in phrases from the tradition and poetry in the Bible and liturgy, would always have *some* truth of applicability in them. The real question was a post-modern one: how could the old man, even having adopted the shaggy look and grandstanding style of a traditional Old Testament prophet, think he could stand *aside* from the situation, shouting "foul — disunity" and not realize that he himself was thereby helping to *create* it? We now knew that even to observe reality was to alter it by our measuring. How much more by our condemnation and reluctance to heal ourselves?

It was nevertheless a harsh message that Fr. Eli screamed at the world, and now at the Abbey itself. Condemn first, pay later. And seemingly no accountability for the prophet himself.

Scary rhetoric. And who would pay? The Abbot himself had doubts about Fr. Paul's taking their sacred chant into such an innovative secular direction in some of the selections of *Godspeak*. Yet he, Malachi, hadn't wanted to stand in the way of spreading the Abbey's faith more effectively and widely. The sheer numbers of CDs and listeners boggled the mind! (Not to mention the increased income they were receiving from the music's sales, he admitted sheepishly to himself.)

But now it seemed that someone had already made a down payment on violence through the desecration of the chapel. Of course, this wasn't the first time the Order had been targeted. Several years ago the sign at the edge of town that pointed to St. Andrew's had been vandalized with satanic symbols, obliterating the name. But that desecration was committed some miles away from their safe sanctuary.

As a psychiatrist, Fr. Malachi understood only too well the dangers of having an unleashed mind mixing among the brothers. But was the perp really Fr. Eli, or someone far more dangerous than an unstable old man who surely couldn't have climbed a ladder to gash out the face of an angel on the chapel ceiling? Or even have made it to breakfast on time if his life depended on it, considering his decrepit, wobbling gait.

But who?

And Fr. Eli was not Malachi's only concern. His trained pastoral eye had observed, on more than one occasion, the glances that passed between the two novices, Sean and Peter, and he wondered at some connection or acquaintance they might have had before coming to St. Andrew's last spring. When Sean and Peter had marched side by side in procession to choir practice, someone reported that once their hands reached out from where they were supposed to be tucked inside their scapulars and touched meaningfully during the Our Father. The young monks were soon given different placements in the line-up, even though the usual rule was that the brothers marched in the order they had come to join the Order.

All of the monks were cautioned by the Rule against "special attachments," senior monks even sleeping in beds between younger monks to deter any breach of decorum, and there was no better time to address any impropriety than when first detected, to nip it in the bud. But with hints of violence afoot in the community, such a potential attachment now seemed a minor, almost nostalgic concern to the overloaded Abbot.

Fr. Malachi's musings were suddenly interrupted by the sound of angry voices coming from the monastery's main hall.

"You told the interviewer that you couldn't find me?!" Fr. Paul's voice ascended to the highest note he had achieved in one of his grand solos.

"You're correct, I *couldn't* find you," Fr. Jean answered quietly. "You weren't in the chapel or the refectory; you weren't in your room. Those people were about to flee this hallowed place by their shirttails anyway. Fr. Eli's prophecies crescendoed into a raving scream at the end of the interview. Didn't you hear? They were relieved to get out of here."

"I was visiting one of the lazy tenors in his room, and, of course, the door was open!" Fr. Paul snapped. "We have another album to consider! You could have made a more thorough search. You obviously didn't want me to be interviewed today. The truth is that you are jealous of me, of my abilities and my fame!" Fr. Paul's tone became overheated and developed more volume as he said the words 'my fame.' "How dare anyone allow that raving maniac to upstage *me!* It's a wonder he didn't crack his 'sword' at them before they left."

"I agree that Fr. Eli trespassed some boundaries, Paul," Fr. Jean said. "However, you're puffed up with pride." A muscle twitched in the smooth butterscotch skin of Jean's usually serene face, and his black eyes flashed anger at the choirmaster. "More than one of the brothers have told me that they perceive jealousy in you when I'm soloist at the Mass." Fr. Jean paused for control. "I am the Prior, Paul, next in authority to Fr. Malachi for spiritual order and confession, and I suggest you go to the chapel and read Chapter 71 of The Rule, especially the part about regarding each other with love and concern at all times."

Fr. Paul's blue eyes were stormy. "You aren't above that rule yourself," he retorted. "I've seen you..."

Fr. Jean broke in. "I see that your arrogance will require a higher reprimand. You should know by now that I want nothing from this music venture but a reasonable percentage of the funds to be sent to our Haitian Project. My people are dying from drinking contaminated water. It has become a matter of survival!" Noticing the cluster of curious monks who had been studying in the library and who had entered the hall at the sound of their angry voices, he spoke more softly.

"The Abbot has told me that your publicist, John Landry, is scheduled to arrive today. Perhaps you can convey your concerns about negative publicity to him. I was merely acting as messenger for those people from the TV station."

Fr. Paul looked contemptuously at the gentle Prior and turned his back on him. The monks standing in the hall made room for him to pass, looking down at the freshly waxed floor, abashed by their curiosity. At the far end of the hall, the maid Cotille stood, waxing cloth in hand, her work temporarily suspended as she inscrutably absorbed the exchange between the two up-and-coming monks.

As Fr. Paul passed the Abbot's office, he glimpsed Fr. Malachi standing in the doorframe, scowling. But the Abbot allowed him to leave the building without reprimand. Silence filled the hall again, and Cotille resumed waxing the floor. Fr. Jean paced the hall for a few moments, his hands swiftly counting the beads on his small pocket rosary; then he turned and entered the Abbot's office.

Fr. Malachi received him with equanimity, passing no judgment on his attempts to counsel Fr. Paul. But now he wondered if he needed to probe deeper than Fr. Eli's rantings, and monks liking each other too well, to get to the core of the community's dis-ease.

ℭℜ

Outside in the parking lot, John Landry, development executive of Classic Universal Recording Company, straightened the knot on his dazzling red tie and spat into the palm of one hand, then smoothed his short-cropped, curly black hair with the dampened palm before he stepped out of his shiny red Ferrari convertible. He walked down the path to the refectory at St. Andrew's, wondering if the gold chain placed over the dazzling red tie might seem a bit ostentatious to the Abbot. But he had actually groomed himself for the eyes of Fr. Paul, the choirmaster. He knew his efforts to impress the star, the lead singer, were pure fantasy; nonetheless, a few mild flirtations with Fr. Paul wouldn't hurt anyone, he told himself. Landry dared not make a move toward the handsome cantor that would offend him. He couldn't risk jeopardizing the money *Godspeak* generated for his company. And surely other hit recordings would follow. Who would have thought an album based on ancient chants by an obscure order of monks would ever hit Gold on the charts and stay there for twelve weeks?

Landry smiled as he approached the refectory and almost collided with the man he sought. Handsome, blond, ascetic-looking Fr. Paul was pacing outside the front door of the refectory as if he had been anticipating the development executive.

"Oh, *so* glad you're here," Fr. Paul began, linking his arm with Landry's.

John Landry, 45 years of age, seasoned by many years of promiscuous affairs with men, blushed a hue as scarlet as the tie he had carefully chosen that morning to dazzle Fr. Paul.

Fr. Paul rushed on. "That son of parents who 'mixed it up,' that voodoo prince from Haiti is the ultimate manipulator," he spat out. He sat down hard on a stone bench along the meditation walkway and gestured for Landry to join him.

"Are you referring to Fr. Jean?" Even the worldly Landry was a bit shocked at the candidness of the monk.

"Who else? The man who dares to think his voice, straight from the chants of voodooiennes, equals anything... anything at all in MY repertoire."

John Landry started at the obvious prejudice in the cantor's words. "What did he do?" Landry looked into the monk's long-lashed eyes and blinked his own invitingly.

"He let Fr. Eli, the mad monk who lurks around the monastery, intercept the TV crew from NOPB and use the time they had scheduled FOR ME to instead interview that crank prophet. Then he sent the TV crew away before I could object and get a chance to promote the ALBUM as was intended. He blew this plum opportunity for *m*... us! He said he looked for me, but I know he didn't. He wants to horn in on my solos and steal the glory of my success!"

John Landry couldn't restrain himself now. He slipped his arm around Fr. Paul's shaking shoulders and left it there. Fr. Paul's petulance only excited him, but the monk thrust John's arm away impatiently. Had the monk begun sucking his thumb, Landry wouldn't have been surprised. He was having a full-blown fit of childish jealousy.

Landry stood, miffed by the rebuff, and turned to leave before his own temper erupted. "You celibates talk a lot about love and compassion but don't seem to be able to endure honest affection very well," he said.

"We're not blind to those who practice the excesses of the flesh and try to manipulate us to do the same," Fr. Paul said loftily.

"Listen, I didn't come here to hit on you. I came to talk about publicizing your work." Landry looked sincere and businesslike as he uttered the half truth.

"You should have accompanied the TV crew," Fr. Paul said, still sulking. "In fact, you haven't been very helpful lately, and I'm beginning to wonder if I really need an official publicist. Fr. Eli didn't seem to suffer from the lack of one." He stood, his tall frame well above the low, wide shoulders of the stocky publicist. "If you had spent more time arranging publicity and less time grooming yourself for 'casual encounters,' this morning's fiasco wouldn't have happened."

Landry compressed his lips as Fr. Paul shot the riposte at him, then words spilled out. "Did you know that there's a long list of aberrations attached to the fear of evil? You should read more than your breviary and the Bible. There's a whole body of writing out there explaining the asocial impulses that build up in a healthy person when the discharge of biological energy, by means of natural sexuality, is blocked. In less technical language, celibacy causes all kinds of mental and sexual aberrations, including anxiety hysteria, psychopathic impulsiveness, pedophilia..."

Fr. Paul interrupted. "We say that in all things God will be glorified. Now, I suggest you get in your little red cruising wagon and take your 'biological energy' back to your office. What I need from the outside world is usually delivered to me without so much messiness as you generate. You can contact me when you really want to talk business." Fr. Paul tightened the cincture around his waist and walked away, leaving the outraged publicist standing by the stone bench, red-faced, fists clenched.

Landry was still standing there when a black limousine pulled up and stopped beside the walkway. The Bishop of the Diocese of the South Province stepped out of the car, pectoral cross gleaming, his face creased in an extravagant, welcoming smile. Come to beg some favor from the Abbot, Landry thought. He shook the portly Bishop's outstretched hand and then pulled away before he could be questioned about Fr. Paul's music project, which the Bishop had reluctantly blessed.

Landry made his retreat from Paul's insults as soon as he could. He felt sick and disgusted that he had just blown his chances with Paul, both personal and professional. *Or had he?* His mind suddenly went into overdrive. Perhaps he could take another, subtler tack?

# CHAPTER V

*God is the name of the possibility I have of keeping a secret that is visible from the interior but not from the exterior.*
                                        ─Jacques Derrida

Fr. Paul, still fuming, climbed the steps leading to the chapel and entered the narthex. Cedar greenery draped the sills of the stained glass windows in the chapel in lieu of flowers during the Advent season, and their pungency filled the church. The fresh scent pleased the choirmaster, and he went immediately to the chancel and sat down on the bench before the 100-year-old pipe organ case. The case, a masterpiece in fine walnut, was reputed to have been built by the cabinetmaker Mallard of New Orleans. He flipped to the music for "Come, Thou Long Expected Jesus," and launched into song. Paul was fond of quoting J. S. Bach: "I play the notes in order, as they are written. It is God who makes the music." His true tenor voice filled the chancel and the transept, and he sang with such vehemence that he startled himself.

When he had finished, he began to play a few non-psalmodic chants without singing. Playing the same melodic phrase in each couplet for several sequences gave him rumination time. He thought about John Landry's accusations and again punched at the keys with unusual ferocity. What did that pompous little fruit know about the lives of monks? Clearly, he didn't understand the specialness of those devoted to the ancient Order of Benedictines, nor did he understand that sexual energy could be spiritually redirected, let alone comprehend what the word 'transcendence' meant.

If Landry couldn't regulate his own physical proclivities then he shouldn't try to dictate others'. He also had no knowledge of the Rule and how it allowed for some frailties, followed by amendment of faults, not to mention the power to distinguish love, real love, from lust. From the size of his waistline, Landry must eat more than the allowance of a pound of bread a day the monks were permitted, too, Paul thought snidely. *"Take care your hearts are not weighed down with overindulgence"* (Luke 21:34), he repeated aloud from the Rule.

One thing for sure, the little hedonist wasn't going to get any so-called 'affection' from him. If Landry wasn't careful, he might find himself out of a job. Fr. Paul fantasized about taking over Fr. Malachi's publicity duties as well. Who needed those interfering intermediaries when Paul knew that his adoring audience really wanted him? Fr. Paul gradually relaxed as he played an excerpt from the classic Advent hymn "O Come, O Come, Emmanuel," and thereby transcended the memory of the publicist's visit.

∞

Within the quiet cell of his office that night after dinner, Fr. Malachi sat thinking about the complications that had taken place in his monastery in one short morning before noonday prayers. The situation was dire, but he still wasn't ready to bring in any outside help. Calling for any official investigation around his monks during this period of unrest could only make things worse, he reasoned. He surely didn't want the local law enforcement people asking too many questions. Their presence was not only spiritually disruptive, they engendered bad publicity for the business of Chant. Now he shocked even himself! When had he started thinking in such a pragmatic, worldly way? Proof enough that he himself needed penance and restitution.

After morning services had ended, he had gone into the sacristy and rummaged in the massive oak cabinets that held altar linens and hangings, silver chalices, and the Communion wine. In one small drawer of the linen cabinet, he kept various prayer cards: the Miraculous Infant Jesus of Prague, St. Anthony, the Blessed Virgin, and a package of cards bearing the image of the adult Jesus on one side and a prayer thanking Him for His close presence on the other. At least one of the burnt cards on the altar had been that of the adult Jesus, and a packet containing that particular card had clearly been opened.

He had locked the drawer only the day before, and when he examined the brass lock closely, he saw that it bore scratches and evidence of an enlarging of the keyhole. Someone had obviously tampered with the lock. Fr. Malachi sighed and closed his eyes. Time enough to begin putting the pieces together. First, he needed to center on his own surrender to God in this predicament. His approach was both spiritual and practical. He always solved problems best when he refocused his mind from the immediate puzzlement and let his intuition sort the mixed pieces of the enigma, suggesting a solution without his overt attention. Of course, he accomplished this while saturating himself in prayer and petitioning the guidance of the Holy Spirit.

Just as he had adjusted his large frame comfortably in his leather swivel chair and set a small desktop timer to measure his period of prayer, Fr. Jean appeared with news of another interruption.

The Rt. Rev. Father, Bishop of the South Province, was outside and had met up with John Landry, the publicist. Fr. Malachi didn't have long to wonder about reasons for the intrusion. As soon as Fr. Jean had made the announcement and settled himself in a side chair, the Bishop appeared in the doorway.

The Abbot rose to greet The Rt. Rev. James Gregory, murmuring words of welcome cautiously. His mind replayed Chapter 33 of the Rule, "All guests who present themselves are to be welcomed as Christ... and proper honor must be shown to all, especially for those who share our faith..." Even meddling superiors and mad monks, he thought ruefully to himself. He had really needed that lost prayer time!

"My dear Malachi," the Bishop said in an unctuous tone. "How good of you to receive me when you're so busy at your work here..." The Bishop glanced suspiciously at the still ticking timer on the desk. As a traditional churchman he was wary of the post-modern practice of an 'emptying' prayer.

"As you can see, I was enjoying a respite from administrational duties. We're honored by your visit. Did you come to preside over Evening Prayers for us?" Fr. Malachi asked innocently. "Please sit down and Fr. Jean will go to the kitchen and request a tray of coffee."

The door suddenly opened and Cotille peeked in. "I saw the Holy Right Reverend Sir come in and thought I might serve him in some way," Cotille said obsequiously, keeping her head bowed.

"Ah, a good idea, Cotille. I prefer that my Prior stay here with us for this little chat. So you can go and get the coffee."

Cotille bowed in an odd half-curtsy before the Bishop and left the room.

Fr. Jean moved his chair beside the Bishop, and the two of them sat facing Fr. Malachi, who remained behind the oak harvest table that served as his desk.

"I won't beat around the bush," the Bishop said. He removed his black coat and folded it carefully, leaving it in his ample lap. "Our Diocese has been named in a suit by a family named Breaux. The allegation is against one of our priests in Algiers, Louisiana. The unfortunate man has been accused of molesting an 11-year-old boy who had been his acolyte for several years. The allegation of misconduct is reprehensible, but I must tell you that it's true. In an attempt to solve the problem, our former Bishop moved this man to new positions three times. The offender received treatment in our best rehab center in the mountains of New Mexico, but I'm afraid his pedophilia is so deep-seated, the physicians had to administer Depo-Provera."

Fr. Jean crossed himself.

The Bishop continued. "I'm afraid we're part of a widespread investigation that has uncovered as many as 3,000 pedophiles in our Church, nationwide. I'm finding evidence that there isn't one solitary bishop in this country who has not dealt with this problem."

"Three thousand?" Fr. Malachi exclaimed. "Where have our bishops been? Why were these men moved around? As a psychiatrist, I know this aberration is incurable. Surely the Bishop had some expert advisors when he made decisions concerning the men with this sickness?"

Dense silence filled the Abbot's office for a few moments. Ignoring the questions directed at him, the Bishop went on. "We must pay restitution for one of our brother's sins against children. I was scandalized to learn that during the 60's when we needed priests so badly, a few promiscuous homosexuals, whose sexual orientations were known by my predecessor, were accepted in the Diocese and placed in administrative positions. Apparently they were unwilling to discipline pedophiles because they were violating their vows of celibacy themselves." The Bishop, with evidence of five o'clock shadow on his chin, unfolded the coat on his lap. He looked hard at the Abbot. "I hope you don't have this problem here with your monks and choir boys."

Fr. Malachi felt his blood rise. "We're a dedicated Order, and we have a reputation for honoring our vows of celibacy because we know how to balance our lives — 'cross, book, and plow,' you know. Why have you come here to question us? Pedophilia is at the top of my list of sexual offenses and has been, even before I became a Religious."

At that moment, the door opened. Again, Cotille entered, carrying a silver coffee service, and set the tray down on the Abbot's desk. She glanced at Fr. Jean, and a smile flashed across her face. Fr. Malachi noticed the strange smile of sympathy, but he was too disturbed about the Bishop's news to ponder the apparent affinity between his Prior and the monastery's maid.

"I need at least two million dollars of your CD proceeds from *Godspeak* to pay off the Breaux family," the Bishop said flatly.

"You might at least have waited until Cotille left the room before making your demand," the Abbot said. "She does understand English." Why did powerful men always think that women, especially those who served, were necessarily deaf and witless?

Fr. Jean stood abruptly. "We're going to pay for a deranged priest's sins with money we made and planned to use to save the lives of dying children in Haiti?" he asked, his dark eyes glistening with tears. "I think the priest should go to prison." He knew Fr. Paul, for one, felt differently. Paul wanted any and all complainants paid off quietly so that the Order could maintain its lofty vocation and continue to sell its — Paul's — music to the world.

Fr. Jean felt that the Abbot should protest this pay-off. The matter was so deeply disturbing and wrong.

"He's already serving time," the Bishop replied. "The parents want restitution."

"We shouldn't be in the business of deploying priests who think they can gain control over their sexual weaknesses and sins by joining the Church," Fr. Malachi said, rising to stand before the seated bishop. "I must personally protest our spending money to save the face of a Church that mocks the image of Our Lord," he stated adamantly, looking his Bishop straight in the eye.

Fr. Jean spoke up: "I offer my humble opinion that we need to do a better job of screening those who wish to enter Holy Orders, particularly since there's no longer a scarcity of aspirants. Perhaps we need sounder, purer leaders to serve on the Commission that discerns the call of these aspirants."

The Bishop ignored this gentle wisdom, and rose abruptly, compelling the others to follow suit, and signifying that the matter was settled and the payment agreed on. Now I'm cornered, thought the Abbot. Any attempt to put a brake on producing further Chant recordings, to stop and reevaluate the community's purpose in light of tempting commercialism had been stymied by the Bishop's co-opting their royalties not even yet earned. At the moment, no further arguments, and certainly not Fr. Malachi's idealism, stood a chance.

Fr. Malachi was not subversive by nature. The holy injunction to obedience ruled his life. But in his mind a process of protest began forming. He decided that the ongoing business of Chant recordings and sales would not include capitulating to his Bishop's habit of paying cover-up compensations. There had to be a way...

Cotille shuffled out of the room. A loud clatter in the hallway startled the men. They scurried out to find her bending over the silver tray from which she had emptied the coffee service, and which she had dropped on the highly polished stone floor outside Fr. Malachi's office. From the doorway, Cotille kept her head lowered to conceal the expression on her face, lest anyone see what she felt about anything she might have heard in the sacred home of the monks... anything at all.

But she was incensed, and her right hand again began its troublesome trembling. Later, after the evening meal, when Cotille was helping the cook dispose of some boiling water in the heavy copper urn, her hand got in the way and she was scorched badly enough to be rushed to the Abbey's infirmary. There, she spent an uneasy night, cursing under her breath, while Br. William, who had bound her hand in gauze and windings, gave her a sedative to calm her down and watched over her throughout the night.

# CHAPTER VI

*With Masses to be celebrated constantly from the earliest hours of the day until the hour assigned for rest [the monks] go about it with so much dignity and piety and veneration that one would think they are angels rather than men.*
 ~Raoul Glaber, monk and chronicler of the Abbey of Cluny in Burgundy, 11th century

fter he entered his pew in the chancel, Fr. Jean bowed his head and covered his face with his hands. He repeated the Jesus Prayer: *"Lord Jesus, have mercy on me, a sinner..."* over and over in his mind while Fr. Paul chanted the short responsories for Compline, the last prayers of the day.

Fr. Jean felt the remorse that comes from indulging his anger—and envy—and pride—and, perhaps, even greed! He reflected on the seven cardinal sins, the 'Saligia,' the same number as the virtues and the notes of the scale, but his capitulation to 'IRA,' or rage, bothered him the most. Anger was a bow to insanity, he chided himself. In the exchange with Fr. Paul, his words hadn't been as harsh as the choirmaster's, but he had secretly wished harm to come to him. There was also his desire to be more important than Fr. Paul, and his willfulness in refusing to compliment the gifted cantor. His sins truly fit the poet Dante's description, "Love of Self perverts to hatred and contempt of one's neighbor."

Fr. Jean prayed for the virtues of patience, kindness, and humility to come into his heart and joust with the deadly sins to which he had fallen prey. What would the old nuns at St. Mary's Orphanage in Port au Prince think if they knew how he had allowed such poison to enter his heart and add to the discord among his brothers? The nuns had taken him in when his mother died during his birth, had selflessly fed and clothed him and trained him in the proper modes of Gregorian chant.

Since he had shown exceptional musical promise, later, Sister

35

Elizabeth, the mother superior, had sponsored him to study music at Juilliard Music Academy in New York City. But she hadn't discerned that he would one day enter the priesthood.

The sight of children in Port au Prince, with their imploring black eyes, dying from drinking water polluted with worms and bacteria, had overwhelmed him every time he returned home on holiday from Juilliard. And before long he knew he had been called to serve them in some way. Passion for the survival of these children powered his call to enter the seminary in New York. But after he had completed his clinical practice work in Harlem, he discovered that he didn't have the physical or spiritual stamina to serve the disenfranchised. He had been sent south to New Orleans, and the Bishop, seeing Fr. Jean lurching toward a breakdown, had transferred him to St. Andrew's.

Fr. Jean continued his mental flagellations and tried to appreciate Fr. Paul's rendition of *Alma Redemptoris Mater*, but anger welled up again. He was a hopeless case, he told himself, but he'd pray for an epiphany of burning love, for a luminous angel to transform him. That angel would give him a ringing voice to bridge heaven and earth and tame the chaos within him and within the monastery.

Singing wasn't just a human activity; it was a spiritual practice that didn't seek approval from the external world. Fr. Jean sighed. Here he was, dreaming, longing for a superior voice again. He buried his head even lower. "To sing is to pray twice," he mumbled, quoting St. Augustine, as Fr. Paul's angelic voice filled the church. Fr. Jean had to admit that the choirmaster was actually the one who had received the ringing voice to bridge heaven and earth. He felt that he, Jean, was more worthy, and therein lay another pitfall of pride.

In a pew behind Fr. Jean, Fr. Eli observed the Prior's distress and withdrew pen and paper from the pocket of his alb, scratching some words on the paper as Compline came to a close.

"O son of man, I have set thee a watchman unto the house of Israel, therefore thou shalt hear the word at my mouth, and warn them from me!" he wrote. Fr. Eli shifted his big bulk in the pew, looking even more uncomfortable in his own skin than usual. His craggy face was set like flint toward completing his unpopular mission in the world, and nothing could now hold him back. *It is for their own good, if only they were wise enough to see it!* He muttered under his breath: *A verbis ad verbera.*

Fr. Malachi left Compline, not only disturbed by the outbursts and disruptions of Fr. Eli, but nonplussed about one of his flock. This time, it was Fr. Jean who seemed to have lost his centeredness. And he depended on Jean, especially now when he needed a clear-headed second-in-charge.

What little Fr. Malachi had seen of his Prior's countenance during Compline, since he had covered his face with his hands, disturbed him. The gentle Haitian was suffering and seemed to be wrestling with some inner conflict. Of course, Fr. Jean had arrived in a similar emotional condition when he first came to St. Andrew's. But within a few weeks after he joined the monks, he had snapped out of a depression he had developed from dealing with the indigent in New York City, he confessed to the Abbot. In fact, Fr. Jean's developing emotional and spiritual steadiness had caused the Abbot to raise him up a Prior, much to Fr. Paul's consternation.

So what now? He guessed it was the argument with Fr. Paul that had caused Fr. Jean to be so disturbed. He'd wait on the walkway for his Prior and get to the bottom of his disturbance.

It was nearly a moonless night. Only a silver sliver was visible, and the night was made even darker by the fact that the grounds of the monastery had no floodlights. Insects whirred monotonously, and Fr. Malachi thought how like the monks' chants their incessant, steady singing was, only the insects never seemed to sleep. Who was to say what sounds or vibrations were actually holding the fabric of the planet together? As his eyes adjusted to the darkness, he could see vague swirls of mist hovering over the lake.

"Were you looking for me?" Fr. Jean asked, touching Fr. Malachi's arm.

"Your intuitive sense is working well, Jean," Fr. Malachi replied. "I saw you covering your face with your hands at Compline and wondered if you were having another episode of depression."

"Always the psychiatrist," Fr. Jean said gently. "And I suppose I could add 'Acadie' to those of the seven deadlies that I've been guilty of committing."

"Oh come now, you know that I think it's more sinful to reproach yourself too much. It's actually a form of self-interest. And what is it I always quote to you from that novel, *The Rector of*

*Justin?* 'Taking one's self too seriously is, after all, the highest form of conceit.'"

"I know that it is, but you forget I was raised by the nuns, and the devil was never far from us, according to them. Some of the Haitian nuns believe that man possesses two spirits: the *Gros Bon Ange*, a spirit that makes the body animated, and the *Ti-Z Ange*, a spirit that renders protection against danger day and night. I know what you'll say, this is dualism, Gnosticism, all heresy."

"You're right. I don't want to hear any of that taken seriously. I know the nuns must have forbidden you to listen to anyone who talked about those practices. Why are you talking about voodoo, with all the truly unwieldy problems the Abbey is facing? It's fine to refer back to your childhood culture, and to take all this *metaphorically*, to allow it to contrast with and illumine your Christian faith, but..."

Fr. Jean touched the Abbot's arm again. "I know. But I take Cotille with her knotted string quite seriously. She must think herself a healer. Surely that's admirable, regardless of her beliefs. I don't see her struggling with '*anomie.*' She just acts. There's something to be said for native intelligence..."

Fr. Malachi was alarmed. "No wonder you're depressed. Surely you're not suggesting going back to ignorance?"

Fr. Jean laughed. "Of course not, I was just playing devil's advocate, I suppose."

"Well, you need to get out of that cultural landscape and into this one right now," the Abbot said sternly. "Now that you've thoroughly spooked me, tell me what's really bothering you."

"It seems that Fr. Paul has become my nemesis. Not only do I envy him, I'm angry with him for being such an arrogant preener." Fr. Jean accelerated his gait down the walkway, and the Abbot quickened his own pace. "You'd probably label him a grandiose personality," he added weakly.

"You know I can't discuss Paul's character or situation with you, Jean. Anything he has told me or I have advised him is protected, just as what you're telling me goes no farther than my ears. You need to go back to the Rule, commit it to memory, Jean, and meditate on it every day, not just when you've been attacked by one of your brothers. I thought you were beginning to live it," Fr. Malachi said wistfully. He stopped walking and motioned for

Fr. Jean to sit down on the stone bench.

"We can probably do this better in my office tomorrow, particularly since we should be in our quarters and bedded down for the night right now. My counsel to you is: try to return to centering on God, repeating a phrase from the Sacred Word and letting yourself relax into sleep. The atmosphere around here lately has become as charged as those wild rantings of Fr. Eli. Maybe that's the source of all this disquietude?"

As soon as Fr. Malachi uttered those words, the two monks heard leaves rustling near an old live oak beside the monastery. Fr. Eli, wrapped in a voluminous fringed cloak, suddenly stepped from behind the oak and began running toward the guest cottage bordering the monastery, laughing maniacally as he ran.

# CRAPTER VII

*Let the monks sleep clothed and girded with belts or cords but not with knives at their sides, lest they cut themselves in their sleep — and thus be always ready to rise without delay when the signal is given and hasten to be before one another at the Work of God, yet with all gravity and decorum.*
≈From the Rule of St. Benedict

Sean and Peter, the two most recent novices to join St. Andrew's, had started meeting surreptitiously to walk together one evening a week and happened to be strolling near the lake when Fr. Eli ran by laughing strangely. The young monks, who had entered St. Andrew's at the same time, coming straight from Juilliard, knew that Fr. Malachi suspected them of having been lovers before they took their vows.

The truth was actually much more complicated than that, and they feared having to confess the true situation to the Abbot—although they believed in their hearts that if only the beauty of their love were understood, it would be celebrated rather than condemned.

There were many historical precedents for such David-and-Jonathan love, 'beyond that for a woman,' yet still chaste. The Sufi poets and philosophers Rumi and Shams, for instance, embodied this love. They knew that "the connection to the Friend is secret and very fragile," as Rumi said.

Sean, a tall, well-proportioned man whose curly red hair had been shorn, radiated vigor and vitality, and he loved his friend Peter passionately. Peter, in contrast, was short and slight, and like many short people, he often showed defensiveness because of his height. However, he waged a daily inner war with his anger and insecurity. He had clear hazel eyes that shone with the effects of his asceticism.

As Fr. Eli raced past them, and they each drew a hand away

**40**

from a loose clasp between them, Peter shivered. "I wonder what he's up to now. I wish that he wouldn't try so hard to appear crazy."

"He has so many demons," Sean replied. "And yet he has seen more of the truth than many of the men here. He *can't* be silent or 'the stones will cry out.' He intuits the subtle and hidden nature of things that most people aren't aware of. It's just that in his ethnic culture too much refinement would be seen as weakness."

"Sometimes I think he's just a mental wreck," Peter said sardonically.

Sean laughed. "Perhaps he needs a spiritual friend, or a real community. We certainly know how it was to live on the fringes of acceptance until we came here."

"Yes, I think Fr. Malachi suspects that we may still be more than spiritual friends, or less than, according to our Rule."

"Until we have an advocate, more understanding, I guess we'll have to continue to nurture each other, and meet like this," Peter lamented, then smiled. *"We are the music while the music lasts,"* he murmured, somewhat sadly, quoting T. S. Eliot. "It could be worse!"

"There seem to be a lot of people out wandering in the dark tonight. We might be seen," Sean said, looking anxiously toward the monastery, unwittingly picturing in his mind a staging of *A Midsummer Night's Dream* with bewitched couples crisscrossing each other in the forest. "It's late, and I think I just saw Fr. Malachi and Fr. Jean head toward the monastery. I wonder what they've been discussing, and I hope it isn't our friendship. I think we should go in before Fr. Malachi becomes even more suspicious of us."

Peter shook his head. "Sean, Sean, you know that the Abbot quotes passages from Aelred's *Spiritual Friendship,* and speaks of friendship as a sacrament of love, a very holy sort of charity. No one knows more about Aelred's dialogues than the Abbot."

"Yes, but he also refers as often to Aelred's view that same sex attraction and opposite sex attraction are equally possible and similarly dangerous to the vow of celibacy," said Sean.

"And?" Peter hurried on. "And then he quotes Aelred's view that friends are guardians of the Spirit itself. 'We carry our friend with us in the deepest part of our being where God is found...' The

Abbot is, as Aelred was, very compassionate about human foibles. He suspects that we're attracted to one another, but somehow I think that he trusts that we'll honor our vows." Peter encircled Sean's shoulder and patted it consolingly.

The two novices decided to make one last stop at the empty chapel to anoint their foreheads with holy water from the baptismal font. Prominently positioned in the narthex were two table displays of the projects the monks were sponsoring with the proceeds from their CD of *Godspeak*.

Haitian handicrafts—banana bark art, small framed folk paintings, and painted metal plaques made from recycled oil drums had been arranged on one table, along with a sign appealing for aid for the Haitian water project. The other table held a simple poster with photographs of several choir boys, advertising the sponsorship of young musicians to attend Juilliard on scholarship, especially those who might have vocations. A slotted box for donations stood beside the display. The two causes represented the respective interests of Fr. Jean and Fr. Paul, a fact that was well known among the monks. Sean glanced over at the displays and gasped. He pointed to the poster and whispered to his beloved friend, "Evil is at work here."

Splashed across the length and width of Fr. Paul's artful poster-collage advertising Juilliard was a large and ugly black "X" along with graffiti of several dicey four-letter words. But most disturbing was the *message* crudely written on the display poster in the same black ink: YOUR NEXT.

The Haitian display was untouched.

The novices were horrified at the desecration of the Juilliard display right there in the narthex. But what they would glimpse next in the sanctuary would make a simple attack of vandalism and its warning pale in importance.

CR

Fr. Eli did not see his own interview on NOPB-TV that was rerun on the evening network and the late night news. He could wait around no longer. The urgency of his mission was weighing him down far more than the actual accumulation of manuscript pages, the last of which he had written, folded, and stuffed into his alb pocket by the end of Compline.

Now he needed the *rest* of his treatise, stored in the side table of the guesthouse bedroom. The flow of revelations coming to him had been steadily waning. The angels had indicated to him that the time to reveal himself as prophet of this community, to truly take Elijah's chair and authority, was nearly at hand!

He surmised that when Sean and Peter saw him come out from behind the oak tree, wrapped in his huge fringed cloak, they were probably afraid that his observation and eavesdropping might lead him to report their liaison to the Abbot. But Eli had bigger fish to fry. A Jonathan-and-David relationship was of no concern to him, except perhaps as an indication that the conditions in the Order had *not* completely deteriorated — yet. If there were a few other supporters of the unity, souls who sought a deeper basis for witness to the world, Fr. Eli would be glad for their good will.

He laughed aloud with guttural hilarity. Soon they would all know!

What would it mean to ascend the prophet's 'chair' and bring an end to the spirit of greed and divisiveness that was poisoning the community? He knew only that it would demand a much larger stage than a local reporting team could cover. He had written his revelations for the masses, addressed to all who had 'ears to hear.'

"Behold, I come. I will make all things known... *What you do, do quickly,"* he muttered to himself, wrapping the folds of the heavy cape more tightly around him and patting the pocket where the newly written sheets of revelation were secreted.

Once he reached the guesthouse and pushed on the door, he had an uncanny sense that someone was looking over his shoulder, although no sounds but the insects' incessant hum pierced the night silence. Had he left the drawer slightly open? He didn't remember doing that, but he must have, as the entire stack of rumpled sheets seemed to be there, several inches thick, tied with a dirty string around the middle.

He reached in and cradled the manuscript like a living thing, in both hands, extracting the new additions from his alb, smoothing the pages flat and inserting them carefully, deliberately. He licked his thumb to grasp and lift the corners of reluctant sheets and line them up as best he could into a stack.

Something was wrong, though. More than just the partially open drawer. There seemed to be a sinister presence in the air, an ominous shadow looking over his shoulder. What manner of devil was it, and from what realm of spiritual darkness, seeking to subvert his mission? He pulled on his ear in perplexity and muttered some Latin words aloud. But he could wait no longer.

He pulled out his beloved katana from its hidden location and clasped it in his right hand. *He who lives by the sword will perish by the sword,* Christ had said. Yet the Apostle Peter had cut off the ear of an opponent of his Lord in the Garden.

Eli's wool cape, stone gray over the red alb that he had donned for this momentous day, was great cover not only for the cold but to protect the pages of written treasure now under his arm, until he could get to Fr. Malachi with his evidence and unequivocal revelation that *he was The One* to right pagan wrongs. It was all evident in his person and his words; the authority had been bestowed on him by God for this very moment in time! *Even if blood were required.*

He left the guesthouse, still feeling the uncanny sense of opposition to what he was about to do. "Get behind me, Satan!" he muttered under his breath. Just so, Jesus had called down those who sought to deter *Him* from *His* mission, denouncing even the Apostle Peter, who later became the great head of this Church!

Fr. Eli's head was filled with so many images and voices, yet he'd be a savior for his own time, ready to stand and fight if need be for the truth that was like a fire in his belly now, as he rushed into the night.

It was by now nearly dawn, he reckoned, though the small slice of moon still reigned as the only light. By it he could see, even through the mist over the monastery pond, what appeared to be a ghost! Not the *loup-garou* that some of the cretins around here believed in. No, certainly a live human figure, yet performing strange actions in the cold water, dipping itself up and down. Was someone performing a pagan mock baptism? Eli could not abide that!

He ambled over toward the shore, deterred on his way to find the Abbot, who was known to be up at the earliest hour, out of all the monks. He glanced again over at the water. This wasn't one of the chosen, but a runt, a wraith, a child? An abomination! Fr. Eli squinted hard but could not determine which.

Suddenly he remembered the Dialogues of the Life of St.

Benedict, their patron, how young Placidus, the holy man's monk, had gone out to retrieve water at the lake, and Placidus, fumbling with his pail, had fallen in after it. The water had carried Placidus away from the shore "as far as one may shoot an arrow." The Holy Benedict was still in his cell, but he knew his monk was in distress. He called for their brother monk Maurus, asking him to go and rescue Placidus. It was then that a miracle occurred that had not been seen since the time of the Apostle Peter himself. Maurus walked right out on the water to where Placidus was sinking, grabbed him by the hair, and brought him safely in. Whereupon Maurus praised Benedict for intervening, but the Holy Benedict would not take the credit, attributing all to the bravery and obedience of Maurus. But the rescued man, Placidus, had settled in his own mind what truly occurred, as he had seen the cloak of Benedict, the Abbot, not that of Maurus, above his head when he was carried to safety.

Fr. Eli smiled at this recollection and thumped his chest at his own blessedness, being in such a line of holy rescuers. He would soon reveal this to all even though this new distraction would tax his waning energy and require great faith. He'd rescue this poor lost figure first!

But Fr. Eli, having forgotten his walking stick in his haste (which was mostly a prop, not a necessity), and trying desperately to hold his manuscript intact underneath his own cloak, then slipped on the uneven rocks of the shore, and never saw the face of the mysterious figure he would have walked out to meet and save.

He hit his head on a rock and lost consciousness.

The bulky stack of papers had been loosely tied with the string. Many had slid down underneath the cloak and were scattered in his path or blown away by the light wind off the water. A few sodden fragments would still be clutched in Fr. Eli's right hand when his body was found late the next day, face down in St. Andrew's Abbey Lake, his cloak nowhere to be seen, but the wide arms of his red alb spread out like a floating angel, or devil, come to an untimely end.

☙

Fr. Paul had stayed alone in the chapel to work on his newest Chant innovations — the deadline for completing them was fast approaching. There were rehearsals to set up, studio hours to arrange. A second, *Godspeak II* album would be just the shot in the arm he needed to unequivocally establish *his* vision for The Heavenly Choir, not that of Jean!

The entire repertoire of historic plainchants was a vast collection of nearly three thousand pieces. Each one, whether a psalm, a prayer, or a hymn consisting of a single melody, would be traditionally sung either by a soloist, the entire choir, or responsively between the choir and Fr. Paul, the cantor.

Paul knew that unless he himself was the designated soloist, his favorite pieces would be the ones performed *responsively*. Yet, he was increasingly finding that some members of the choir balked at his innovations, accusing him of stretching the definition of 'chant' itself! They just didn't appreciate his genius.

It was not as though essential chant had *ever* been consistently sung in a strictly mathematical, stilted style. Any single-line melody always offered opportunity for subtle variations in its tempo and musical quality. It could be *personalized*. That's what Paul was doing, he assured himself.

He, Paul, had something new to affirm to the world: sequences without pre-set boundaries. Chant could *rock*. And Paul's "extreme chant" was bound to wake people up to what the monks' way of life was really about: Life in all its vividness and promise. He locked his eyes on a point on the far wall, spacing out for a few moments, envisioning his own face on TV, in magazine feature articles...

There had been controversy over adaptations and changes in chant through the ages, of course, and various times of straying from simplicity, with the result of orders such as the Benedictines of the Abbey of Solesmes, France, in the nineteenth century, striving for decades to return chant to its established medieval forms.

Paul scratched the tip of his pen unsurely on the paper, playing with examples on the composition sheet of some of his wilder departures, notes that he knew he could reach easily, but involving intervals that challenged the traditional order of progression. Why should he have to conform to the least savvy among the choir, as though everyone had to be on the same page with every recording? He had heard them whispering behind his back, and he knew dissension could prevent him from getting the best work out of the men. He thought momentarily, with disgust, of Fr. Eli and his earlier crude criticisms. At least he didn't have to include the old crank!

He, Paul, was an *artist,* and that meant pushing the envelope, despite the warnings of Fr. Jean, and perhaps even the Abbot's growing doubts about Paul's musical independence.

He crushed a sheet of staff paper into a fist-sized ball and tossed it toward the altar in a pique. Then he started spanning the organ keys using both hands, pulling out stops and blasting the complex chords more forcefully than was needed, as though to defiantly implant a deviant musical sequence in the chapel air. This was his choir! His future!

# CHAPTER VIII

*To you I lift up my soul: in you, my God, I place my trust;*
*do not let me be ashamed; neither let my enemies exult over*
*me...*

—*Ad te levavi, plainchant*

The next morning Fr. Jean was scheduled for kitchen duty with Fr. Paul, and he dreaded the encounter. Anticipating the conflict that was sure to follow, he decided to go to the chapel before anyone else was awake. He needed to pray that he'd remain calm when he had to wash Fr. Paul's feet before they served together. "Both the one who is ending this service, and the one who is about to begin, are to wash the feet of everyone... Rule 36," he chanted to himself as he entered the narthex. Focusing on his own inner struggles, he failed to see the ruined Juilliard display off to the right of his line of vision.

Fr. Jean yearned for meditation time alone, but he also needed to alert Fr. Paul. He had glanced at the notepad by the reception hall telephone and read that the TV reporters were coming again this morning for an interview with the choirmaster. There would be time for Paul to talk to them before he and Paul began kitchen duty. Jean, feeling penitent and conciliatory, was even willing to do more than his share to allow Paul this privilege!

The lights had been turned off, and the dim interior of the chapel seemed almost menacing to Fr. Jean as he approached the chancel. In the half-light, he barely made out an unmoving figure sprawled before the altar rail and trembled as he neared the stretched-out form. Fr. Jean stepped in a pool of bright red blood, nearly slipping down, and looked down at the slashed, almost beheaded figure of his dead brother, Fr. Paul. He gasped and ran down the aisle, moaning "help" at each step he took. When he reached the steps leading out of the chapel, he stopped to grasp the wooden rail dividing the steps, doubled over, and vomited.

Wiping his mouth with the sleeve of his alb, he stood erect and looked into the puzzled eyes of his intuitive master, the Abbot, who had also been driven to pre-dawn prayers and who had fortuitously appeared at the scene.

"He's dead," Fr. Jean said flatly. "Dead, and I wished him to be so."

"Just stop that right now," the Abbot said. "Who's dead and where?" He stepped widely around the pool of vomit on the step and put his hand on Fr. Jean's arm.

Fr. Jean led the Abbot into the chapel and up the aisle, stopping before the rigid figure at the altar rail. He noticed a crumpled page of paper beside Fr. Paul that he had overlooked when he first glimpsed the body.

"My Lord and my God," the Abbot said. "Looks like someone used a sword to cut his vocal cords straight through!" He crossed himself, turned away from the sight of blood splashed everywhere in the sacred space, and picked up the edge of the crumpled note with a corner of his alb, opening it awkwardly with his own hem to avoid making prints. The page of staff paper he unfolded bore the usual penciled-in notes, no doubt some of Fr. Paul's recent composition work modifying the chants. But overlying the work were several large, dark X's, the scrawled letters crudely negating the musical work on the sheet. The Abbot peered intently at the black marks on the crumpled paper. He placed it back where it had lain.

"We knew Fr. Paul was working late in the chapel — but this — what does it mean? The formation of the words seems too crude to be Fr. Paul's, unless they're some kind of renunciation of his own work," he thought aloud. "NO MORE what? No more writing of chant or changing the sequences into 'rock' semblances, or no more living with the doubts? I wonder if Fr. Paul was suicidal? Surely not. Someone else could have come in on him. The chapel door was unlocked, as usual. I often come here in the night to pray myself," he said. "Don't touch anything. We must call the police." He started back down the aisle of the church, flinging a remark over his shoulder to Fr. Jean, who stood immobile before the dead body. "I just pray that neither Fr. Eli, nor anyone else of our own, has sunk to the level of murdering fellow monks."

When Officer Dan Murphy called Detective Zelda Wagner to report that a priest at St. Andrew's Abbey had been murdered, Detective Wagner felt no surprise that one of the Religious at the monastery had been nearly beheaded. Zelda Wagner wasn't shocked at clandestine happenings in the Roman Catholic Church. She was agnostic and had become even more suspicious of the Church since the discovery of rampant pedophilia among the clergy.

She sighed and fluffed her short champagne-colored hair, opening her worn black purse to extract a small gold compact. Although her makeup was intact, her blue eye shadow evenly applied, and her thin lips bled a violent red, she decided to apply the stick of Revlon 'Really Red' more thickly. She frowned at the crow's feet surrounding her hazel eyes and the wrinkles on her forehead, visible signs of a temper easily provoked. At 50, she felt jaded, unmoved by eccentrics and menacing personalities, even by murder in its most bizarre forms. So many years had passed since she had flown off to Niger with the Peace Corps to save a world from poverty and disease and married a Nigerian who worked with the Corps. She had spent one unhappy year trying to meet his irascible demands before he ran off with a woman of his own culture. She returned stateside, feeling undisturbed by man's inhumanity to man and strangely fearless.

Crime was now her métier, and her only bow to civilized life was her devotion to music. A former male opera singer who had undergone a sex change came to Detective Wagner's apartment at night and gave her voice lessons, accompanying her on the baby grand piano which the detective rarely played, using it only to strike chords to initiate the scales she sang. The huge showpiece piano filled half the living room of her small apartment. It was the detective's only extravagant piece of furniture, and she referred to it as a 'homecoming mistake.'

Detective Wagner's favorite opera, of course, had been composed by a musician with her family name—Wagner. At the end of lighter days when she wasn't forced to pursue investigations at night and before her voice coach arrived, she often played recordings of Richard Wagner's tapestry of loud sounds in operas that were German to the core. 'The Ring,' which featured the wild horsewoman of the air, Brünnhilde, particularly stirred her. She identified with the dissonance in Wagner's work and understood his desire for resolution. Her work, like the composer's, could be identified as dissonant—a vocation contrary to conventionally acceptable professions. Yet, sometimes she longed for more harmony and conventionality.

Detective Wagner's soul had been shaped by the subtlest of attitudes toward the disenfranchised in a struggling country rife with dark moods, and an indigence that her hard-boiled team of detectives couldn't begin to envision. She knew that, behind her back, team members called her Little Miss Tough Teats.

She dressed in a forest green sweater with long green leather skirt and black leather jacket, which had been her winter attire for the 15 years she had worked among the derelicts and mad dogs occupying the underbelly of Marksville, Louisiana. She wore elegant black leather boots, which added to her 5' 2" height, and she knew her team members also called her a Nazi goose-stepper behind her back. Little Miss Tough Teats, Nazi goose-stepper, she was diffident about their name-calling, choosing to regard the insults as indications that they were fond of her. She knew the men on her team wouldn't hit on her because she lacked an essential delicacy that was as necessary to human females as pheromones were to other animals in attracting mates.

Detective Zelda Wagner entered the main room of the Crime Scene Unit, calling out orders in a thick southern drawl as she walked through the cluttered office.

"Detective Bronson, see if you can't get Dr. Patin at his office and, if not, call The Camellia Bar. Tell him to meet us at St. Andrew's Abbey and to sober up along the way. Someone has attempted to behead a priest."

Detective Earl Bronson settled the wire arms of smudged glasses more firmly on the ears of his balding gray head and stood, his overweight frame towering above his petite boss. He saluted her derisively.

Detective Zelda Wagner strode through the maze of battered wooden desks in the Detective Division of the Marksville Police Department, calling for Detective Jason Bell, head of the Identification Unit, and within five minutes she had assembled a parade of crime scene experts who silently followed behind her.

"Don't be intimidated by all those medieval robes and pious

manners," she instructed the team as she walked. "This is a grim reaper scene. The dispatcher reported that the Abbot said someone used a sharp instrument to execute a real O. J. Simpson swipe at the priest's vocal cords. By the way, the dead priest is that famous composer and vocalist who recorded a contemporary version of Benedictine chants..." her voice trailed off. Only a music lover would know about the chants, Detective Wagner thought. She doubted that her team members listened to anything except Hootie and the Blowfish or other 'happy rock' tunes from their teenage years in the 90's. Perhaps they didn't listen to any music. She hadn't ever heard one of them whistle a note from music that was either popular or classical. They were stodgily pragmatic.

As the petite detective exited police headquarters, a black and white Ford sedan swerved over to the curb. Detective Bronson bowed before her mockingly and opened the rear door on the passenger side for her, then got into the front seat alongside the driver, a rookie police officer.

"St. Andrew's Abbey," he directed Patrolman Carter, "and no stops for anyone. Let that old fart Patin find his own way."

◌◌

After discovering Fr. Paul's body, Fr. Malachi had remained in the narthex and sent Fr. Jean outside to await the police. He stood, head bowed, at the side of the holy water font, his mind churning with cogent memories, not of Fr. Paul, but of his wife's suicide. Prayer was impossible for him, except for the ejaculation "Jesus," which he repeated over and over while dark memories inundated his thoughts.

His wife Virginia had always been fascinated by the British writer, Virginia Woolf, because she suffered from similar bouts with depression. From Fr. Malachi's reading, he had discerned that Virginia Woolf's ordeal had been more agonizing than his wife's episodes, or so he had thought before his wife took her own life. She didn't have the urge to write, and he often berated himself for not encouraging her to compose more than the few journal pages he prescribed for her to complete daily.

Fr. Malachi felt constriction in his chest as he recalled the disillusionments his Virginia had suffered, the vocation she had attempted to fulfill as a nurse and, later, as a caseworker, before her delicate psyche became so disturbed that she quit working for any agency. Unlike her favorite author, Virginia Woolf, his wife possessed no wit and power of visualization, showed no interest in using her mind to create, and eventually she even ceased reading anything. Finally, she took to her bed.

As a psychiatrist, Fr. Malachi had dared to think he could treat her, and prescribed lithium; but unbeknownst to him until after her death, she had disposed of the medication and merely sunk into a deeper depression.

"I feel madness overcoming my mind," she told Fr. Malachi the night before she committed suicide. "There are terrifying voices in my brain telling me to leave this world."

Alarmed, Fr. Malachi had decided to seek the help of an outstanding woman psychiatrist the following day. At dawn, after a sleepless night, he had gone into the kitchen to make coffee, and as he poured the strong, dark-roast brew into Virginia's favorite ironstone mug, he heard the explosion of a gun. He found her in the bathroom where she had filled the tub with water, a considerate last act, he thought immediately, for she had known the bath water could be drained off, leaving little blood to clean up. No stones-in-the-pocket drowning like Virginia Woolf for his wife. A perfect shot had pierced her chest, and she had died instantly. Atop a black silk sheet in the bedroom was a brief note: "There were too many demons. Unlike Virginia, I never found my moments of being."

That tragedy had catapulted Fr. Malachi into the seminary, away from violence and mental aberration, or so he had thought at the time. Who would have dreamed that a mad prophet would appear at the monastery and that a murder would occur in the quiet sanctuary of their chapel?

Fr. Malachi cleared his throat and looked up the aisle at the image of the crucified Christ hanging over the altar. He began to pace back and forth in the narthex, and as he walked, he presented himself with suspects: Fr. Eli, the outsider with the grandiose personality? Fr. Jean, his beloved assistant who seethed with jealousy toward Fr. Paul? John Landry, the publicist, whose interest in Fr. Paul bordered on unrequited love? A fan of *Godspeak*, perhaps a schizophrenic whose hate had centered on Fr. Paul because he had been rebuffed by the gifted vocalist at a concert? His mind discarded all of them. In his work as a former psychiatrist, Fr.

Malachi had trained to become a skilled analyst. Yet, along the way, he had missed the signs pointing to his own wife's suicide. Was he dismissing the strong destructive passions of these major suspects too quickly? Had he lost his ability to analyze when he began to trust a higher power and vowed to become a celibate? Had his prolonged periods of solitude led him to illusions about the next world where he might meet his wife again? Had long-term celibacy started to dull his natural gift of spiritual intuition?

Fr. Malachi thought about the early Church Father Athanasius and the theologian Thomas Aquinas, about the desert mother Syncletica and of Mother Teresa (who had lately been exposed as a depressive, God forbid!). And then there was Aelred, who had helped him come to a Christian understanding of how to relate to other humans. "Here we are," Aelred had written, "you and I, and I hope a third, Christ, in our midst." And here he was, Abbot of a monastery, uttering Jesus' name, and in the same breath blaming himself for the death of a fellow priest *and* his wife's death simply because he hadn't fully acknowledged Virginia's act as a desperate one for which *she alone* was responsible. What responsibility might he have ignored that had caused the death of Fr. Paul? And lurking in his conscience was the thought that he had contributed to a soft-peddling of pedophilia by acquiescing to the Bishop's demands. He chided himself for self-conceit and stopped pacing, suddenly recovering his own equilibrium.

"Just in the nick," he muttered aloud as Fr. Jean entered the narthex and announced that the police had arrived.

# CHAPTER IX

*[When] the pitcher is broken at the Source, then shall the
dust return to the earth as it was, and the spirit shall return
unto God who gave it.*

#### ~ Ecclesiastes 12:6-7

etective Zelda Wagner marched past Fr. Malachi up the
aisle to the altar with her retinue trailing behind: Detective
Bronson, her assistant; Bart James, a member of the Crime
Scene Division, and Herb Tarver, a crime lab technician. She stood
over the inert form of one of the world's most gifted experts on
chant and said to everyone present, "What a blasted waste!" And
a moment later, asked, "Where's the coroner? He'll probably show
up crocked, but how much expertise will he need to pronounce
this one nearly beheaded by a long-bladed instrument, perhaps a
sword? Hell, I could get over the causeway to New Orleans in the
time it's taking him to make an appearance."

Two patrolmen stood beside the bloody body, awaiting orders.
Since only Fr. Jean and Fr. Malachi were in the chapel, the officers
had told the two priests not to leave the chapel and hadn't corralled
them into a contained area.

Detective Wagner set her crew to work dusting for fingerprints
and searching for hair samples. The photographer began snapping
pictures of the corpse and the blood that was spattered across
the altar, attempting to get a clear image of the pattern of the
bloodstains. Detective Wagner glanced briefly at the crumpled
piece of paper beside the corpse, turned and walked down the aisle,
halting before Fr. Malachi. The Abbot, standing erect, regarded
her with a questioning look and fingered his pocket rosary. He
remained outwardly stoic, a handsome icon of the Church.

"Your name?" the detective asked.

"Fr. Malachi. I am the Abbot of this monastery," Fr. Malachi
said crisply.

"I hope none of you have touched anything around the body," Detective Wagner said flatly. She searched the Abbot's impassive face.

"I'm sorry. I'm afraid I opened the note with the hem of my alb," Fr. Malachi said.

"And why would you do that?"

Fr. Malachi shrugged. "I'm privy to all of the priests' writings," he said simply.

"Well, I'd hardly call this a 'writing.' You may have disturbed fingerprints. However, on this stone floor, as cold and dry as it is, the print on the paper would probably vanish quickly anyway. We'll dust, but you may have destroyed evidence." Detective Wagner peered more intently at the Abbot. "Are you the one who discovered the body?"

"No, I'm not. My assistant, Fr. Jean, found him and came looking for me just as I entered the chapel to say my prayers before Mass." Fr. Malachi beckoned to Fr. Jean who was sitting in a back pew observing the exchange between the detective and the Abbot.

Fr. Jean stood as Detective Wagner addressed him. "What were you doing in the chapel?" she asked.

"I had also come in to pray before doing kitchen duty, and when I approached the chancel, I saw him lying there. I almost slipped in the blood when I got to the altar."

"Yes, I noticed a few shoe prints. Is it the custom for all of you to come to the chapel preceding your regular morning service? Or is there some disturbance going on here that you're trying to resolve by praying?" Detective Wagner searched the priest's face for signs of discomfort.

"We often pray before we pray," Fr. Jean said. "It's our calling to be in constant prayer."

"What time did you enter the chapel?"

"About 5:30."

"Did you see anyone else in the chapel doing this constant praying thing?"

"No. It was very early. Most priests who want to pray before the service don't appear before 6:00."

"And you saw no one on the path leading from your quarters to the chapel?"

"No, I didn't. As I said, it was early."

"What kind of relationship did you have with Fr. Paul?"

Fr. Jean flinched, then plunged into the truth. "We quarreled at times. He was often arrogant about his giftedness. Just yesterday, I allowed a TV crew to interview a visiting monk, Fr. Eli, when Fr. Paul was scheduled to be featured instead. I couldn't find Fr. Paul anywhere at the time, and the crew decided to put the spotlight on Fr. Eli. Fr. Paul then accused me of trying to subvert his career. He also accused me of envying his talent and fame."

"And were you jealous of him?" Detective Wagner snapped. She was now fully engaged.

"Yes, sometimes I was, but I had remorse for feeling that way. I try to abide by Chapter 71 of our Rule."

"Which is?"

"Essentially, we're to regard each other with love and concern at all times."

Detective Wagner smirked and began walking toward the altar, flinging over her shoulder, "Someone didn't pay much attention to that rule. I'll question you further, later. You can return to your constant prayer, but as the person who discovered the body, you've become very suspect, I might add." Her drawl echoed in the silent chapel where Mass wouldn't be celebrated while the crime scene remained sealed. Returning to the altar area, she complained vigorously to Detective Bronson about the absence of the coroner and the need to determine postmortem lividity.

"I know the degree of hypostasis doesn't always give us an accurate picture of the time of death, but we could get an estimate if the old fart would show up," she said, although she was aware that the coroner would appear after he had finished his morning drinking. Reprobate that he might be, he wasn't only the chief medical examiner, he was an excellent forensic expert. She relied on him despite the fact that he was lurching toward senility.

❧

At 7:00 on a chillier than usual Louisiana morning in December, Dr. Alphonse Patin, Chief Medical Examiner for St. Helena Parish, appeared at the chapel of St. Andrew's Abbey very drunk. He pulled in next to a gleaming red Ferrari parked in the lot next to the chapel. When Dr. Patin got out of his car, he stumbled and would have fallen if a patrolman standing in front of the church hadn't stepped forward to steady him. The coroner, a disheveled, bald-headed man, had reached his sixth decade and now seemed to be well on his way to early dementia via the bottle.

"They're looking for you," said Officer Ben Wingate. Detective Wagner had dispatched him to corral all the monks and any person who appeared on St. Andrew's property. Wingate, a veteran patrolman of 30 years, had never taken a drop of alcohol while he was on duty and felt deep disapprobation for the shuffling, ruddy-faced medical examiner. A vegan and natural food advocate, the patrolman worked out on his lunch hour daily and boasted a fit body, which was part of his plan for regulating a stressful life. Before he could voice his opinions about the impropriety of drinking on duty, John Landry, wearing an obviously expensive overcoat, tapped him on the shoulder.

"What's going on here? Why are all the monks gathered on the walkway?" the publicist asked, putting on what he considered his innocent, doe-eyed look of concern.

Without replying, Officer Wingate turned to his sidekick, Patrolman Rowan Miller. "Take Patin inside and see if you can't get him to walk to the altar without falling down. This is a monastery, for god's sake," he said irascibly.

He returned to the publicist's questions. "A priest has been murdered. No one's allowed to enter the chapel or to leave the grounds. What's your business here?"

John Landry stiffened. "Which priest? When? Oh dear!" Landry put his hand to his throat unconsciously and patted his pocket where a sheet of paper he had secreted there suddenly felt like dangerously concealed evidence. Before the patrolman could answer, the red-haired commentator and hippy photographer from the New Orleans Public TV station, who had earlier interviewed Fr. Eli, appeared, whispering loudly to each other when they saw the morose-looking crowd.

"Obviously you smelled news," the patrolman said. "No media, folks. The Abbot wants no reporters here at this time." He spoke falsely, presumably on the Abbot's behalf, and was about to embellish the story when John Landry interrupted.

Landry waved the TV team away. "I'll talk to you later," he said. "One of the monks has suffered a mishap. I should be back in my office by noon." The curious TV commentator and photographer withdrew without challenging Landry. But as they walked away, the red-haired commentator muttered "they're always protecting the Church, even the police."

Landry glared at Officer Wingate and demanded, "See here, I had an interview lined up with my client, the cantor, Fr. Paul. Can't I get in to see him?"

"I don't think you want to see him at this moment. He won't be chanting anymore. He's a very dead cantor. Vocal cords cut, end of song." The patrolman said the words curtly, staring suspiciously at Landry. "You may be a suspect, for all I know. Where were you in the early morning hours?"

"No, no, no!" John Landry moaned and promptly sank to the ground.

"Damn drama queen," Officer Wingate said. "Looks like we're going to be busy sobering up drunks and reviving suspects," he grumbled to one of the monks standing on the walkway. "Come here and wake up this fancy dressed wimp and have him join the rest of you. I need to go in and inform Detective Wagner we've added another suspect. Don't any of you go off the property. I'll send Patrolman Miller out to make sure you don't."

Two monks who were huddled close together on the walk looked at him and smirked. They never "went anywhere off the property" as the officer suggested they might. Obviously, the patrolman had never been near a Benedictine monastery.

Patrolman Wingate left when the novice Peter rushed over to John Landry and began speaking into his ear. Landry opened his eyes and fluttered his eyelids several times as he gazed into the deeply set eyes of the handsome Religious smiling down at him.

But the reaction to Peter's lovely, concerned face was more instinct than sense. In fact, when Landry had been wandering around the Abbey grounds hours before, keeping out of sight, he had seen the diminutive Peter and his taller consort Sean go into the chapel in the early morning hours. The pair had left abruptly, probably having found the body, he now realized. Landry decided to keep that little fact to himself in case it could help get his own neck off the block later. *Calculation* was as commonplace to Landry's personality as flirtation or breathing.

On several occasions, Landry had noticed a small figure darting around corners, just ahead of the eye, ducking behind trees or outbuildings. In the misty dawn, the publicist's excitable temperament and credulity had even made him think that perhaps the Abbey itself was haunted. Now there was reason to fear.

Poor, lovely Fr. Paul was gone. It couldn't be possible! Surely they wouldn't think that John Landry would do that angel voice any harm, in spite of the rebuffs Fr. Paul had inflicted on him. Landry had always survived by staying above the fray and keeping his eyes on the gain for himself. For now, keeping silent, and holding onto a certain piece of paper — he tapped his vest pocket — was surely best.

◌

When Patrolman Miller reached the altar with Dr. Patin on his arm, Detective Wagner ignored the swaying coroner. As if he had been anticipating the arrival of a corpse since daybreak, Dr. Patin went straight to the side of the dead man and bent over him.

"We need to find and interrogate this Fr. Eli person," Detective Wagner said to the patrolman. "Fr. Malachi will show you to his cottage. You can search there and scour the lake area. I've seen this self-appointed prophet on TV, and he looked pretty demented. See if you can't turn up a long-bladed knife somewhere. Get Wingate to help. I'll be along after I question some of the monks outside." The patrolman bobbed his head up and down in agreement with her commands and hurried down the aisle.

As Detective Wagner turned to follow him, Detective Bronson approached her, dangling a plastic envelope before her.

"You've found something?" she asked, peering through the plastic at a small bag containing what appeared to be shards of whitish and grayish rubber. "Where did you find this?"

"There are bits of it all over the altar area, even a few in the center aisle. I'd guess they were shed from something the murderer was wearing. Too small for fingerprints, but the material should be a match to something, other than the note and the blood, that is."

"Keep searching, Bronson. Even monks who dress and look like cookie cutters have to have some distinctive differences. We've got to figure out who 'cut short' Fr. Paul's late night vigil with the slice of steel."

Detective Wagner turned and strode down the aisle. As she approached Fr. Malachi, she announced, "You can return to your office for awhile. Just don't leave the grounds. Show the patrolman where Fr. Eli's cottage is located before you settle in your office."

"I hardly ever leave this property unless I visit the Bishop or have a meeting."

"Well, I suggest you call him immediately and tell him there's 'murder in the cathedral,'" she said ruefully. "I've asked Patrolman Miller to look for Fr Eli, and Detective Bronson will assist me with the questioning. Are there any cooks, maids, gardeners, or handymen who haven't shown up outside?"

Startled, Fr. Malachi blurted out, "I don't think they're implicated. They usually leave the premises after supper and cleanup."

"You don't seem to believe anyone here is implicated. No matter about what time they leave every day. They have keys, don't they?"

"The maid Cotille has keys to many rooms, though we hardly ever lock anything but the sacristy. That's the room here in the chapel where the gold vessels and Communion elements are kept." He touched his own key ring on his belt. "Actually, I heard that Cotille was laid up in the infirmary overnight with a burnt hand—cooking accident. But I think she's up and around again this morning."

"She needs to be found and to join the group outside." Detective Wagner turned and went to the front door of the chapel. Sighting Officer Wingate, she crooked a gleaming, red-nailed finger at him. Wingate approached his boss eagerly.

"Search for a maid and the cook, and before you do that, send in that person sitting on the ground and the monk attending him," she told the patrolman.

"Do you want to interrogate the monk standing beside them too?"

Detective Wagner glanced at the trio on the grass by the walkway. "What's wrong with the one on the ground?"

"He fainted when he heard about the murder. Or that's his story."

"A good one for starters," the detective said. She observed the ministrations of Peter and the anxious look of Sean, who hovered near the pair. "Looks like a gaggle of gays," she said sardonically as she reentered the chapel.

Overhearing the conversation, Fr. Malachi winced at her flagrant prejudice and whispered to Fr. Jean, "You stay in the chapel in case she has any more questions. She seems to be totally lacking in empathy for any of us."

Fr. Jean glanced at his mentor and nodded, then resumed his rosary.

After the Abbot had directed the two patrolmen to Fr Eli's empty cottage, he went to his office and sank into the chair facing his perpetually tidy desk. This place was an 'anchor' for his life, but now even it was barely holding him together in this messy situation. He felt distinctly queasy. Murder before breakfast. Sounds like an Agatha Christie title, he thought, crying "My Lord and my God!" aloud again. His body felt heavy, unwilling to move, and he sat motionless for a few moments, trying to recover a quiet mind and spirit. He reached for the telephone and dialed the Diocesan office. The Most Reverend, already disturbed about sexual molestation among his flock, would need a tranquilizer after this announcement, he surmised. However, when the administrative assistant to the Bishop answered the telephone, he told the Abbot that the Most Reverend was in prayer. The Abbot delivered the succinct message that a monk had been murdered at St. Andrew's and hung up when the assistant gasped.

What next? he thought. The monastery had surpassed the seven deadlies in this latest happening. Where had he gone wrong as an Abbot? "Let the abbot always remember that at the fearful judgment of God, not only his teaching but also his disciples' obedience will come under scrutiny. The abbot must, therefore, be aware that the shepherd will bear the blame wherever the father of his household finds that the sheep have yielded no profit..." St. Benedict's Rule reverberated in his mind. And, then, "...the abbot must know that anyone undertaking the charge of souls must be ready to account for them. Whatever the number of brothers he has in his care, let him realize that on judgment day he will surely have to submit a reckoning to the Lord for all their souls, and indeed for his own as well..."

Fr. Malachi cradled his head in his hands and moaned aloud. After a few agonizing moments, he lifted his face to recite the "Our Father." When he had finished his recitation, he stood before a crucifix hanging on the wall beside his desk and genuflected. Logic slowly returned to his mind. He would mentally examine each one of his beloved flock and discern whether any of them had possessed sufficient rage to cause them to become temporarily insane.

During his preliminary examinations of those desiring to submit to the Rule, he had turned up no one with homicidal tendencies. A singular exception to the monks now at the monastery was the visiting monk, Fr. Eli, who was slightly unhinged. No, this monk was more than *slightly* unhinged. The old man was an anachronism, full of war language, and Fr. Malachi hadn't seen any evidence of the real prophet Elijah's healing powers in his latter-day namesake. Fr. Eli seemed to be fond of disconnected bloody passages and retribution, unable to live in the present, and governed by a God that demanded sacrifice. Elijah the Tishbite of the Old Testament had been a voice of challenge, a prophet who dueled with Baal worshipers on the hillsides of Mt. Carmel in an effort to bring them to a notion of one God. Fr. Eli, in contrast, didn't seem to know whom to challenge or why. He antagonized nearly everyone and was just short of psychotic, in the Abbot's opinion.

As much as the Abbot disliked the idea of volunteering information about Fr. Eli to tough-minded Detective Wagner, he couldn't, in good conscience, discard the idea that the mad prophet, who had often brandished a sword, *could* unravel and kill someone. He'd meet with the detective later.

Suddenly feeling illuminated by the Spirit, Fr. Malachi decided to search Fr. Paul's room for clues to the murder before the 'buzzards' began to invade it. He left his office and climbed the stairs to Paul's cell on the second floor, walking softly and feeling as though he was trespassing the law just by entering the dead cantor's room. The monks' private quarters were usually off limits to anyone, even the Abbot, and exchanges between monks were to be carried out in the hall or the library, or out of doors while they got their daily exercise in the open air. Intimacy between monks invited severe reprimand; in some cases, abbots found it necessary to expel the offenders. Fr. Malachi had noticed Fr. Paul defying this rule of privacy by meeting with members of his choir in their rooms and had overlooked it, because he knew that Paul's work on the new CD of chants required precise instruction of choir members.

The door was open, and he entered it cautiously. Paul's room, unlike the other 'cells,' was spacious, but in keeping with monastic rule, contained no adornments. It had no window hangings, and the uncarpeted oak floor, due to Cotille's vigilant care, gleamed with a golden sheen. However, the room was defiantly untidy. Music manuscript pages littered the floor, covered the surface of a large mahogany desk and the unmatching oak table beside a single metal cot, badly made up with a rumpled Madras print bedspread. A large armchair with a bold green and red striped slipcover faced two windows that overlooked the lake glistening in the distance. Curiously, the room wasn't a book-lined sanctuary. A breviary and an illustrated volume of *Lives of the Saints* on the desk comprised the musician's 'library.'

Fr. Malachi withdrew a pair of white cotton gardening gloves from his pants pocket and pulled them on. He began riffling through papers on the desk, trying to ignore his feelings of disapproval about the many notations of alternative chants boldly scrawled on pages of music script. He worked swiftly, anticipating the entry of the police, even the fierce Detective Wagner herself.

He approached the bedside table where a few sheets of plain typing paper had been turned over so that the writing was hidden. His heartbeat accelerated as he read the almost-illegible handwriting of Fr. Paul:

"Jean, I've noticed that you have formed a clandestine alliance with Cotille, and I saw you walking with her near the lake rather late at night a few nights ago. I'm thinking that the Abbot would want to know about this impropriety. Perhaps we could meet in the chapel tomorrow night after Compline, after everyone has bedded down? Concerned, Paul."

# CHAPTER X

*We believe that the divine presence is everywhere and that in every place the eyes of the Lord are watching the good and the wicked... Let us consider, then, how we ought to behave in the presence of God and his angels.*
    ⁓The Rule of St. Benedict

D etective Wagner allowed Fr. Jean to leave the chapel after he had prayed himself into a state of dryness, but she had again cautioned him to remain on monastery property. He decided to take a walk and went around the chapel toward the field that had been a summer garden, a plot now planted in cabbages. The wind was out of the north, and when he became cold, he sought shelter under the dilapidated, tin-roofed farm shed that housed an ancient John Deere tractor. The sides of the shed were open to the brisk air, and he settled in a back corner behind the tractor where two large bales of hay afforded warmth. He sat down next to them on the dirt floor of the shed, feeling the need to ponder the secret meeting he and Cotille had managed only a few nights before the murder. The afternoon of this meeting, Cotille had stopped him in the hall of the administration building, where she was doing her eternal waxing, and told him she needed some advice about voodoo, that she thought she had been 'crossed.' "Someone has placed a spell of bad fortune on me," she said simply, head lowered as usual, all the while polishing the already glossy floor.

Without informing the Abbot, Fr. Jean agreed to meet her at the farm shed that night after all the priests had gone to bed. When he was certain that Fr. Malachi had turned off the light in his office, a signal that he had retired for the night, Fr. Jean had gone to the shed, flashlight in hand. Cotille had emerged from a heavy mist, holding a Coleman lantern in one hand and a small black satchel in the other. Before he could speak, she had spilled the contents of the satchel on the floor of the shed and lifted the lantern so that he could view the objects she emptied on the ground: a clay doll, a bottle of oil, incense, four white candles, a black candle, and four pieces of white paper marked with Cotille's name in large black letters.

"You need to uncross me," Cotille said. "My cousin told me to get someone who knew voodoo and God to uncross me. She said a traiteur won't do anything because traiteurs are afraid of magic." Cotille lifted her dark eyes, looked into Fr. Jean's, and hastily crossed herself.

"I don't believe in voodoo," Fr. Jean said. "But I do know and worship the one God. There's enough evil in the world without trying to conjure up mischief between persons. I'll anoint you and pray over you, but that's as far as I'll go." Fr. Jean spoke kindly but firmly to the disturbed woman standing before him.

"But you know the ways. They're very similar to traiteur ways."

"No, they're not. Traiteurs heal sickness and are usually strong-practicing Roman Catholics. Their healing powers don't conflict with our doctrine."

"But my soul is sick. Someone has 'crossed me.' If you don't help me with equally strong voodoo, I'm afraid the devil will be unleashed."

"Nonsense, go and see a traiteur. Their power is from God. They say prayers just like we do."

"They only cure warts, hernias, liver problems, anything that melts away when the moon wanes..."

"Cotille, I can anoint you and tell you to recite the prayers you were brought up with, but I can't get involved in voodoo just because you've allowed yourself to believe in such magic as someone 'crossing' you or wishing bad fortune for you."

Huddled in the shed, Fr. Jean now recalled the string of French words Cotille had spat at him with a viciousness he hadn't perceived she possessed, and shuddered in his haven beside the hay bales. Cotille had picked up the objects on the ground, tossed them into the satchel, and run away, the lantern swaying and flickering ominously in the thick mist as she departed.

Suddenly, he felt the cold more keenly and got to his feet. Glancing around the shed, he noticed an article of clothing on the rusty seat of the tractor. He moved closer to the ancient machine and picked up a small black leather jacket, a child's piece of clothing. When he held it up, a clay doll, resembling the one Cotille had shown him, fell to the ground and broke into several pieces. He stooped to retrieve the pieces, folded the jacket over them, and left the shed, jacket under his arm. After he took the items to his room, his conscience directed him toward the chapel and the hard-nosed Detective Wagner, as he knew he had probably uncovered an important piece of evidence. As he walked toward the chapel, he met the Abbot on the path.

"Jean, I've been searching for you. The Bishop has arrived and is waiting in my office," the Abbot announced.

They walked at a brisk pace and became engrossed in quiet conversation, not glancing even once toward the shore of the lake where Fr. Eli's body lay, face down in the water, his prophetic voice silenced and his robes billowing around him.

☙

John Landry had recovered from his histrionic 'swoon' and the abrasive questioning by Detective Wagner, and was on his way home, where he intended to stay the remainder of the day. He felt wretched and had to change clothes. He had appointments to meet and plans to make for more media coverage about anticipated changes in the choir, after this tragedy. But first he needed sleep and time to recover from the death of his star cantor.

Before the horrendous demise of Fr. Paul, he had remained resentful about the talented cantor's rebuff of his advances. But he had decided he needed to be around the Abbey while the TV crew worked this morning. He knew where his bread was buttered, and Fr. Paul's personal rejection of his flirting hadn't deterred him from wanting to appease the source of supply. Inwardly he seethed to the point of an explosion at the arrogant priest's condescension and condemnation of him. Yet, that morning, after a conflicted, uncomfortable night, he just had to show his face. He hoped the muffler at the neck of his overcoat had hidden any light traces of whisker growth, since he hadn't shaved this morning. What a fool he had been, he fumed. Curiously, he now felt dispassionate about the death of Fr. Paul. He knew he must concentrate on the future and attempt to repress the memories of the dreadful tragedy, news of which would soon set Marksville buzzing. But the piece of evidence in his pocket that he had retrieved from Paul's room, before word of the murder leaked out, complicated things.

Landry loved the town of Marksville and his California style stucco home in the Sawmill Pond Subdivision not far from the site of an abandoned sawmill on the St. John River. It was the site of the old Green farmhouse where, in the early 20th century, the melancholy wife of a lumber baron had lamented the lack of musical concerts in the region. Landry often thought about her isolation in the piney woods, from dawn to dark, while her husband cut down all the statuesque long-leaf pine surrounding their farm and beyond. It was rumored that Green had cut down so much of the forest, one could stand on the porch of his farmhouse and see the town of Marksville five miles away. The apocrypha surrounding the old sawmill characterized Mrs. Green as a talented violinist who formed her own orchestra of husband and two brothers-in-law so that she could enjoy a bit of culture in the evenings. Landry lived half a mile from the Abbey and another half mile from the old sawmill, and each time he crossed the wooden bridge by the St. John River where the woman had often stood, musing, perhaps, about sailing away, a palpable melancholy overcame him.

He could have gone to The Camellia Bar, but the thought of his usual 'Gentleman Jack' whiskey didn't appeal to him as comfort because he knew he'd drink too much and would feel worse later on in the day. Just across the old bridge, he pulled over beside the riverbank and rolled down the car window to let in the pine-scented air and to feel the river breeze on his flushed cheeks. The old river and another adjoining one had drawn city people from New Orleans for years, and they had built second homes or vacation cottages alongside its banks in the early 1900's. Earlier, several mineral springs in the area had provided ozone waters for those recovering from a yellow fever outbreak in New Orleans during the late 1870's, and by 1891, Marksville had gained attention nationally as one of the healthiest spots in the United States.

The downtown area of Marksville was designed in 'ox lots,' squares within squares, a unique architectural design in which each block in the middle of town had an open center approachable by an alley from two streets. With the help of a grant from a historical preservation foundation, the downtown had become a thriving historic district. Landry had perceived the potential of the town even though the downtown had been boarded up during the oil bust of the 1990's. The subdivision in which he lived carried a hint of resort living, and some of the 19th-century cottages with New Orleans style patio gardens had been moved onto the site near the St. John River. The parish seat of the most affluent parish in the state, Marksville had grown more than he had dreamed the town would develop, and the Chant CDs recorded at the Abbey seemed to be a natural outgrowth of a burgeoning population's interest in the Arts. He envisioned a large music center at St. Andrew's that would lure musicians from all over the world. After all, a coloratura soprano from Marksville had performed in European opera houses.

Landry sighed and rolled up the window of his car. When the murder mayhem died down, he'd speak to Fr. Jean about the gentle Prior's taking Fr. Paul's position as the lead cantor. He was surely the logical choice. Murder or no murder, the music must go on.

⚭

Sean and Peter stood before Detective Wagner, both trying to avoid her probing, sea green eyes. Peter's body was stiffly erect, clearly in a stance of defense, but Sean's shoulders drooped dejectedly.

"OK, you two, what's your story?" Detective Wagner asked.

"Story?" Sean countered politely.

"Where were you on the night this sword fight took place? *That* story."

Sean spoke again. "We were out walking near the lake for a few minutes after Compline. We often do this in the evening."

"With the Abbot's blessing? Meeting in the dark?"

"Well, no... but the meetings are innocent of wrongdoing. We know the Rule..."

Peter interrupted, speaking truculently. "Before you start a background check, you might as well know that I have a record."

Detective Wagner searched the novice's face and surprised him by continuing the line of questioning she had begun. "I'll get to that later. While you were having this clandestine meeting in the dark, did you see anyone?"

"Fr. Eli ran past us laughing about something," Sean said. "And..." Sean glanced at Peter, then hurried on. "We stopped at the chapel to anoint ourselves with holy water in the narthex."

"Fr. Eli again? Where is this monk? Never mind, we'll turn him up. What is the narthex? I'm not Catholic," the detective said impatiently.

"The entrance where the Holy Water font is. We saw that a table display in the narthex had been desecrated. The poster asking for sponsorships of music students to attend Juilliard had been defaced with a black 'X' and a message that said 'YOUR NEXT' had been marked on it." Sean paused, his face pale with anxiety. "We saw someone lying near the altar and were too spooked to investigate. We ran from the chapel and returned to our rooms." Sean put his hands into his alb pocket to stop them from trembling.

"You didn't approach the altar? We have collected evidence of footprints, so speak up if you went that far into the chapel," Detective Wagner said tersely.

"No, no, we ran away," Sean protested.

"Easy enough to match shoe prints," Detective Wagner said. "And now's as good a time as any to ask about your record, Peter." She turned to Peter, looked into his angry eyes and waited for him to speak.

Peter stiffened, but he kept his gaze level with the detective's. "When I was a teenager, I was sent to a correction facility near Angola, but my record was expunged. My father was an abusive alcoholic who tried to stab me with a kitchen knife that I managed to turn on him to avoid death. The social workers have records of a long history of his abuse and molestation," he said bitterly. "He was so evil that dogs ran from him when he walked down the street."

"Where did this happen?" Detective Wagner's voice softened, but her assistant, Detective Bronson, who stood at her side, knew that she'd be unwavering in her interrogation.

"New Orleans... the Quarter... on Esplanade. My mother was a bar maid. He was a bum, scum from the backwaters of Algiers who lived off my mother."

"Where is she?"

"Dead. Heart failure. Worn out from heart woes and abuse. Failed hope. No faith. No family. Natural causes from unnatural living. You can look all of this up."

"Does the Abbot know about your past?"

"Only that I once lived a life of excess and debauchery in the

French Quarter and am now sincere in my desire to live by St. Benedict's Rule." Peter's shoulders slumped, and he seemed to diminish in height as he stood before his interrogator.

"I don't know about this grand Rule, but I'm sure that St. Benedict didn't include anything about murder in the Rule," Detective Wagner said sarcastically. She sighed and observed the pair. "I think it's probably for your own good that you discontinue your evening walks, but then, I'm not the Rule troll here. Just a suggestion. We'll check out your story. Meanwhile..."

She was interrupted by Officer Wingate who yelled from the narthex, "Another body by the lake, Detective Wagner. You're needed outside."

"Damn," the detective said. "Two in one day. Do we have a serial killer at large?" She hurried down the aisle, stopping at the font in the narthex to shout at the two novices still standing in the chancel. "Don't stray too far. We may have more dead cats to unearth."

As the two detectives exited the chapel, an ambulance pulled up in front of the entrance. The pasty-faced driver approached Detective Wagner. "We're here for the body," he said laconically. "Inside," Detective Wagner said. "You can take this body on to the mortuary, but as soon as the coroner does his work on another one we've just discovered, we'll be calling you back. Just an alert that you're not done here." Without waiting for an answer, she brushed past the driver and strode toward the lake where Fr. Malachi and the Bishop stood, watching Officer Miller drag the drowned prophet ashore.

# CHAPTER XI

*See deep enough, and you see musically; the heart of Nature being everywhere music, if you can only reach it.*
≈**Carlyle**

.

Fr. Eli's body looked smaller to Fr. Malachi than it had when the prophet was alive and fully animated, waving his arms and spouting his denunciations at the air, or at anyone who would listen.

After noting the prominent contusions on both temples, Detective Wagner told the patrolmen to bag the body. "Either he fell twice on these rocks," she said, pointing downward, "or someone finished him off after he fell."

Fr. Malachi crossed himself. In that moment he thought not of Holy Scripture, but, of D. H. Lawrence's plea for a spirit of respect "for the struggling, battered thing which any human soul is." In time he'd know how to feel. That is, if they got through this.

"Lots of sodden pieces of paper were floating around his upper parts, but we couldn't recover any of it worth testing," Officer Miller reported.

*Where were his cane and cape, his sword?* Fr. Malachi wondered.

The others glanced around, and Officer Miller ran to snatch up sheets of paper that the wind had blown away, one against a tree trunk, others scattered down the shore away from the monastery.

"What's an octave?" Officer Wingate asked, as he peered at the scrawl on the sheet they now associated with the revelations Fr. Eli had boasted about.

Officer Wingate read aloud: "Benedict divided each day into an octave of services, separated by seven intervals of monks' activities. The movements of the celestial spheres obey the *musica mundane*; the daily life of the monks follows the *musica humana*; and their voices, the *musica instrumentalis. As above, so below.* Each constituted an octave within an octave, and all were governed by the same principles. *Per ardua ad astra.*"

"What's that mean?" the officer asked.

"Fr. Eli was fond of quoting Latin," Fr. Malachi volunteered. "It means literally: 'Through difficulties to the stars.' It's calling us to love the highest. He was working on more than condemnations, it seems. The whole monastic experience is based around the octave, or the interval of seven diatonic degrees... "

"Huh? I thought this guy was an imposter who claimed to be some dead Old Testament figure come back? What's this about, anyway?"

On another page that Patrolman Miller had handed Fr. Malachi, the prophet had written: "After a certain period of energetic activity, work becomes tedious and tiring, moments of fatigue and indifference enter into feeling; instead of right thinking a search for compromises begins; suppression, evasion of difficult problems. But the line continues to develop though now not in the same direction as in the beginning... If, however, at the necessary moment, that is at the moment when the given octave passes through 'an interval,' there enters into it an 'additional shock' which corresponds in force and character, it will develop further without hindrance along the original direction. — P. D. Ouspensky."

Malachi noted internally that the old monk had equated the trajectory of daily life at the monastery with the beauty and integrity of the progression of notes in chant itself. He wondered what Eli had in mind for injecting as the 'additional shock'? Then he remembered his own paralyzing shock at the brutalized body of their chief singer of chant, struck down at the holiest spot in the sanctuary. Fr. Malachi started to reevaluate: *Surely someone with this much understanding would not so maliciously interpret an abstract theory of unity, however ancient and credible the theory. Though Fr. Eli always talked about a return to oneness and what it would cost to accomplish it.*

Detective Wagner sighed at her staff's ignorance about the wonderful plainchants, which still mattered to her, a music aficionado, *culturally* if not religiously. "Just gather it all up, guys. I'll go over it with the good Abbot in his quarters while you hand over the body. I want the full report. You've got my cell number. And find all the pages of this *evidence* that you can."

"Father, can we meet in your office now?" Detective Wagner

interrupted Fr. Malachi's thoughts. The Abbot began leading her meekly toward his office sanctuary, where he believed that tangled thoughts and lives could begin to be put right, through prayer and guidance of the Holy Spirit. But now he put one foot in front of the other perfunctorily, bearing sadly diminishing hopes of such an outcome. He stopped abruptly, remembering that the Bishop was waiting for him in the administration building.

"I must meet with my Bishop, who is waiting there right now, but as soon as he leaves, we can get together, " Fr. Malachi explained, hoping she would understand the priority of Church protocol even in the face of such an event. She frowned, but put out her palm to symbolically push him on.

CR

The Rt. Rev. James Gregory squirmed in a straight-backed chair in the Abbot's office, his discomfort exacerbated by the recent violence at St. Andrew's monastery.

"I don't believe the so-called murder of Fr. Paul is an inside job," he told the Abbot. "And I want to believe that Fr. Eli, as uncoordinated as he was, slipped on the rocks, hit his head, and drowned." He grimaced with distaste.

"Malachi," he continued, "you have sat and watched while the Order and God's work here were slipping away from your control! It's bad enough that you allowed that old reprobate *Eli-Jah* to be resident here for extended weeks — and let him draw attention to his antics and accusations through the media! But now *we will all be a laughingstock,* not to mention the fact that you've stirred up increased suspicions of what *really* goes on behind cloistered walls!" His anger was palpable. Yet, as usual, he seemed more concerned about *image* and *perception* than the real lives of the monks, even though two of those lives had just been irrevocably lost. Fr. Malachi was shocked at the lack of pastoral care they were receiving, and even more so at the Bishop's seeing the two deaths as inconvenient for *his* purposes! *Lord, have mercy*, he prayed silently. *And help me find the words...*

Fr. Malachi knew his superior, and how shrewdly Bishop Gregory could act in situations in which his logic was indisputable. The Abbot felt his own disadvantage keenly. Perhaps he *had* waited too long to act, lingering, indecisive, like some clerical Hamlet, contemplative but impotent while a hotbed of vicious emotions and murderous intent was festering, rotting within St. Andrew's. But he had to agree with the Bishop's conclusion. He too felt that none of his monks were capable of such brutality and destructiveness. This was pure evil, a bloody catastrophe that could threaten all of their future in that place.

Fr. Malachi's heart sunk. How could he, with such lofty intentions, and all his training in human nature, have gone so wrong? And how could he begin to restore confidence in the hearts of his quaking monks, who no doubt felt violated by the police's probing interviews and couldn't admit, even to each other, how frightened they were for their *own* lives, if, indeed, a killer were loose on the grounds. He started into attention again.

Bishop Gregory cleared his voice, and continued: "And now that our star cantor has been, ah... eliminated. We have to face the fact that sales of CDs by The Heavenly Choir may plummet."

This was beyond sacrilege! Fr. Malachi was screaming internally. Was there no limit to the man's crassness? He crossed himself as though to ward off any further hurtful accusations and dug his fingernails into his own left palm.

Then he somehow wrested back his inner control, and in a spirit that should have been a reproach to his Bishop's coldheartedness, countered:

"Death under any condition is heartbreaking enough. But realizing that such hate is rampant on our premises, are we even worthy to send our music out to the world under these conditions? How can we even *think* of it right now? Two funerals to prepare for in what should be an Advent 'quiet,' a period of waiting and anticipation for the three levels of Christ's coming to us—past, present, and future. What an irony. All this has come crashing down during weeks that should have prepared us for the demands of our vocation in the coming year. Instead, we are back to beginnings, maybe even having to defend one or more of our own against outside accusations..."

The Bishop sighed heavily and shifted in his chair. "Indeed. Well, we have much to discuss. I've told my assistant that I'll be here for the morning at least, so perhaps you should order coffee and prepare for a long session," the Bishop answered. "With the chapel commandeered by the police, Mass is out, I suppose, anyway."

His tone seemed oddly threatening, and the Abbot experienced a quivering sensation in the bottom of his stomach. "I'll call Cotille," he said, getting to his feet. He was irritated when he opened the door and found the maid polishing the floor in front of his office. "The Bishop wants coffee," the Abbot said tersely, closing the door before Cotille could acquiesce.

The Bishop stood and stretched his large frame. "Before Cotille returns, I want to mention something that has troubled me each time I visit here."

The Abbot felt his stomach quiver again.

"It's about the two novices, Sean and Peter. I've been informed that they're together more than they should be, and my assistant has completed an investigation, which reveals that they were likely engaged in homosexual activity when they lived in the Quarter. I wonder if one of them might have had a crush on Fr. Paul and became enraged when Paul rejected him, and the other one was complicit. Do you think they're really suited to the life of celibacy in this monastery?"

The implication of the Bishop's barely veiled threat struck the Abbot with startling ferocity. "You want them to leave the monastery? They're innocent of your suspicions!"

"Well, if you should continue to increase the proceeds from the CDs, despite any setbacks, and help us pay for the Diocese's pending sexual harassment lawsuits, perhaps we could give them more time to show us their devotion to their vows..." The Bishop touched the fingertips of his soft hands together, unconsciously forming an enclosure — or a trap, Fr. Malachi thought.

Clearly Gregory had his own agenda in mind for this meeting, and was simply riding roughshod over Fr. Malachi's doubts and questionings about the wisdom of continuing the music business as usual.

The Abbot, incensed, tried to moderate the tone of his voice. "From the beginning of their stay here, they were warned about the gravity of the obligation of chastity, which they pledged to uphold, and I trust they will do so. I also trust that you aren't suggesting moral blackmail."

Cotille opened the office door, silver tray in her hands, one of them still wrapped in gauze. When she startled the men, the Abbot raised his normally benign voice. "You should announce yourself in some fashion before intruding into our private conversation, Cotille."

Cotille mumbled "sorry" to the Abbot and placed the tray on his desk, head lowered and the expression on her face as impassive as ever. She shuffled out of the room, and the Abbot poured cupfuls of steaming dark-roast coffee for the Bishop. His acidic stomach warned him not to fill his own cup.

He addressed the Bishop again. "If you've decided that we must continue the music ministry," he conceded, "I think the adverse publicity might actually spur sales of the CDs. I'm not concerned about that at the moment, and you are my Bishop, so I'll certainly comply with your request for half the proceeds. However, I hope that you'll honor my request to fund the Haiti Project. Clean water is needed there more than ever since the last two hurricanes. The children are dying before they reach the age of three because of polluted water, as I've told you, and we need money to purchase equipment and hire technicians to travel there and teach the Haitians how to purify the water; to renovate an orphanage there, also. The needs are interminable. We must help these people." Fr. Malachi felt his stomach churn as he spoke, but he went on. "The Rule, Chapter 4, is very explicit about this: 'You must relieve the lot of the poor, clothe the naked, visit the sick... go to help the troubled and console the sorrowing.'" Even, or especially, under these circumstances, he thought to himself.

"I'm not asking you to turn your back on Benedict's Rule," the Bishop said waspishly. "But we can't allow false accusations or greedy suits to destroy the Church either. There is the larger body to consider, not just your monastery and its charitable projects. We won't argue about this anymore, Malachi. It's 50-50 on CD proceeds, and I might add, I expect the profits to at least equal those that we received before these two horrendous disturbances. I expect you to wrest back control of your Order's life and witness, beginning now. And I suggest you put Sean and Peter on a short leash." The Bishop delivered his ultimatum and began to tap his right foot on the slate floor.

Then the Bishop looked at his watch and got to his feet. "I have other appointments today, and I must confess that I'm not only burdened, I'm deeply horrified at the happenings in this holy place.

I choose to believe that the deaths weren't what the police call an 'inside job,' but the activities going on here certainly indicate a need for spiritual direction, penance, and prayer. Malachi, I suggest that you do your own sleuthing to clear the Church of any complicity."

"I'll do my best to discover the perpetrator of Fr. Paul's death and the cause of Fr. Eli's apparent assault and drowning," the Abbot said wearily. No matter how much soul-searching agony it requires of me, he added to himself. The Bishop might have been horrified about the murders, but he seemed to have no remorse about the spiritual murders his pedophile priests had committed, Fr. Malachi thought, inwardly fighting for self-control.

The Bishop gave a blessing and marched out, face rigid with disapproval, slamming the office door to emphasize his disapprobation.

His departure was followed by a rap on the door, and before the Abbot could invite anyone in, Detective Wagner, flanked by Detective Bronson, opened the door.

Detective Wagner remained standing. "I've waited long enough to tell you we've uncovered no evidence to speak of, other than the folded note, the bloody footprints, and those rubber pieces. We still have some strong suspicions about Fr. Eli, as he was observed making threats that could have been aimed at Fr. Paul. But the handwriting on his manuscripts in no way matches the note next to Fr. Paul's body or the words on the display poster. We are working on a timeline of both men's movements through the night. I've already been given some eyewitness accounts. Fr. Eli's drowning complicates the picture, unless he killed Fr. Paul and was then hit on the head by someone else who was also involved. We'll return with warrants to search the rooms of both monks tomorrow and have sealed off the chapel, as well as the area where the mad monk was found. You'll have to hold services somewhere else for a few days." Detective Wagner looked at the Abbot's dismayed face. He had expected as much. But it affected his spirit. "Do you have any suspicions about anyone who might want to murder Fr. Paul? Other than Fr. Jean, his undoubted rival," she added. "Or perhaps John Landry? Or, tell me, who was especially incensed or threatened by the old monk's accusations or presence?"

"Well, we all had cause to be offended by Eli's rantings at various times," Fr. Malachi admitted. "He thought we, as an

Order, were on the wrong path, apparently because Paul changed the sequences in the traditional chant, and broke with tradition. Or maybe Eli was jealous of the attention Paul got in the media. He certainly retaliated by telling his own side of things, whenever a camera was near, but I think he *was* sincere. I saw some of the manuscript pages..."

"What *was* that all about? That is my other question, Father," Detective Wagner sounded genuinely interested.

"Well, I haven't had time or opportunity to look at the pages more closely. But Fr. Eli, for all his bluster and gruffness was a self-taught scholar. He certainly projected arrogance, and even threat in his manner. But it was because he took the role of prophet seriously. He obviously felt God had sent him here to announce something, but he never got around to making his 'stand' like the biblical Elijah, who proclaimed the true God's power and saw the destruction of pagan altars..."

Detective Zelda Wagner held up her hand. "Well, that's more than I guess I need to know. So in your opinion, was Eli-Jah capable of murder? And wouldn't he want a crack at Fr. Paul, who represents Chant, your album *Godspeak*, to the world?" (What impudence to call it that! she thought to herself.)

"No, I don't think he was capable of murder," the Abbot answered after a moment of silence. "He sometimes carried a katana, a Samurai sword passed down through his family, which he hung on his belt, but he never hurt anyone. I guess we were used to his so-far-harmless eccentricities. He was even observed doing a sort of ethnic dance at the local pub, ah, in the last week or so. He wasn't totally decrepit. But murder, no. I don't think that sword was found, was it?"

"First I've heard of it. He owned a katana? Whoa, now we do have some serious considerations here. What about Fr. Jean? Didn't he have the most to gain by getting Fr. Paul out of the way? Isn't he next in line, as someone told me, to replace Fr. Paul as choirmaster and rock star?"

"I'm convinced Fr. Jean had nothing to do with these tragedies," the Abbot protested. "And I don't perceive Landry had a motive to kill Fr. Paul. Paul was money in the bank for Landry."

"I understand one of the novices had a record," Detective Wagner persisted. "Is it possible?"

"I don't believe that this is an inside job, and neither does our Bishop," the Abbot remonstrated. "We do believe in an orderly life here. This has been our Order's lifestyle since its inception when Italy was in a strife-torn state in the 6th century. We are Christocentric and put the love of Christ above all else."

Detective Wagner shrugged and admonished the Abbot: "No one should leave the monastery until we say so; stay put and try to reestablish that order you say you had accomplished before the dead bodies turned up." She turned and was gone before the Abbot could tell her good-bye.

# CHAPTER XII

*There is a way between voice and presence where information flows. In disciplined silence it opens. With wandering talk, it closes.*

**~Rumi**

Fr. Malachi needed the silence of the chapel. He could hardly bring himself to think about entering the sanctuary where he'd view the sealed-off scene around the altar. But he felt drawn to a space where he believed the angels dwelled, despite the murder on their doorstep.

After the police departed, he sat quietly for a few moments. He felt keenly the responsibilities of being the Abbot of St. Andrew's. He picked up a copy of the Rule of St. Benedict lying on his desk and flipped to Chapter 2, The Qualities of An Abbot. His attention was captivated by the phrases: "If he has faithfully shepherded a restive and disobedient flock, always striving to cure their unhealthy ways... the shepherd will be acquitted at the Lord's judgment. Then, like the prophet, he may say to the Lord: I have not hidden your justice in my heart; I have proclaimed your truth and your salvation but they spurned and rejected me. Then at last the sheep that have rebelled against his care will be punished by the overwhelming power of death..." That's retribution, not consolation, Fr. Malachi thought ruefully.

Fr. Malachi couldn't believe that someone in his flock had been capable of murder, that any of the monks could have committed that most heinous act right under his nose, consorting with demons beneath a ceiling painted with angels. He was steadfast in his beliefs about the traditional seven deadly sins, always pointing his monks to Proverbs and reciting "A proud look, a lying tongue, hands that shed innocent blood, a heart that deviseth wicked imaginations, feet that be swift in running to mischief, a false witness that spreadeth lies and that soweth discord among brethren..." *Lord, have mercy,* someone had committed *all* of these sins and was in need of redemption!

Had he been blind to his fellow monks' behavior? Had one of them been guilty of all these hateful things while he was busy mentally defending the Abbey's reputation as a charitable institution because it appeared the monks were enjoying prosperity and popularity?

Fr. Malachi left his office, and found that Fr. Jean had been lingering, perhaps waiting to see him after the Bishop, then the police, had departed.

Fr. Jean gingerly touched him on the arm. "I need to talk to you, Father," he whispered.

Fr. Malachi's heart stopped. Was he about to hear a confession of murder? Surely not from the gentle Jean in whom he had placed so much trust.

"I need to confess to you something about Cotille," the Prior said simply.

Startled, the Abbot invited him in. "Please speak up, Jean. I've heard and seen so much in the past two days. Help me put it in perspective. Do you know anything about who is behind this evil?"

"Strange pieces of a nasty puzzle. No, I'm not sure that what I have to reveal is relevant, but... Well, it's rather bizarre, even for Cotille. Several nights ago, Cotille came to me, asking that I 'uncross' her, a word that implies the removal of a spell of misfortune someone has placed on her. She didn't reveal the person who had done this, and I refused to cooperate with any voodoo rite. She had brought along a satchel containing various spell-related objects, and when I refused to uncross her, she put the objects into the satchel and ran away," Fr. Jean said.

"This took place two days ago?" Fr. Malachi asked, wondering if that had something to do with why Fr. Paul never found Jean and thus didn't get to deliver his note about meeting Jean in the chapel, the night of Paul's murder. He glanced at his desk drawer that now held the note, taken from Paul's room, and frowned at his Prior.

"She was agitated, and I felt sorry for her. She seemed so lost."

The Abbot interrupted. "I know about *crossing* and *uncrossing*, Jean. And I've read about the Dahomey religion in Haiti and how animistic it is. All that conjuring, *gris-gris,* blood drinking... and fornication, I might add."

"Well, sometimes voodienes practice both voodoo and Roman Catholic rituals and claim both are paths to God. If they live a good life and don't hurt others, we shouldn't worry," Fr. Jean said lamely. "I had to tell you about Cotille. If any voodoo objects are found around the grounds, I wanted you to know that I have kept my word and am not tampering with any of that."

"I'm glad to hear it," Fr. Malachi responded. "Voodoo in this state once thrived in the Storyville brothels in New Orleans and still persists in the cypress swamps near this city, as well as other parts of southern Louisiana. Voodienes in the U. S. send novices to Haiti so that they can be trained to become priestesses in voodoo practices, as you know. Haitians believe that their belief in this sorcery helps fight off misery and death. It's black magic, plain and simple, and is one of the reasons I'm concerned about our mission in Haiti. Many of these Haitians have mixed satanism with voodoo rituals and have fostered it here."

"All the more reason for the Church to increase its presence in Haiti," Fr. Jean countered.

"After our talk about this earlier...!" The Abbot felt himself getting hot under the collar at this new revelation. "I'm surprised that you've even dared to discuss this subject with Cotille. You know the old theory about the power of suggestion, and that if faith can heal, despair can kill. We know of cases where death has been caused by a person experiencing extreme fright and despair because of belief in voodoo. I forbid you to meet with Cotille about this hocus-pocus again."

"Yes, Father. And you do believe in my innocence?"

Fr. Malachi gazed into his Prior's imploring eyes and responded, "Yes, I do. But Jesus also told us to avoid even the *appearance* of evil. If this comes out, our detective friend might have a very different take on it. I hope there is nothing to connect you with the chapel at the time Paul was attacked?" Fr. Malachi asked, testing his Prior.

Fr. Jean thought back to the events that had led up to the murder and his discovery of the body. Would his explanations hold up, or would he bring disgrace on his Order, when all he really wanted was to serve?

Fr. Malachi reluctantly launched into another subject, dutifully following up on the Bishop's orders: "With regard to the CD sales, which are crucial to all of us, Jean, I request that you become the lead cantor, and, of course, that you discourage anyone... anyone at all, from discussing voodoo at this monastery. I don't intend to fire Cotille, but I will make it clear to her too."

After Fr. Jean left quietly, Fr. Malachi felt himself even more drawn to the sanctuary, to the consecrated atmosphere of the chapel. As he paced beneath the trellised meditation walk, he felt his heart lift. He was truly glad to be a monk and that he hadn't become the rector of a parish church where God's business was mostly done in parish halls—youth group sessions, church suppers, Knights of Columbus meetings—where parishioners sat in metal folding chairs and when the evening ended, worship was folded up and put away in musty closets. Here, the sacredness endured in continuous chants.

Suddenly, the sour notes of the murders evaporated, and he experienced a moment of intuition as the fragment of a psalm passed through his mind: "Cast me not away from thy presence, and take not thy holy spirit from me." Propelled by the Unseen, his feet turned away from the entrance to the chapel, and he walked around to the side of the church. He approached the sacristy door and stood before it a moment, contemplating the wooden box, similar to a mail chute, that had been nailed shut. The chute had been used to receive the offerings of worshipers who lived on nearby farms and who in earlier years had deposited bulky produce as their tithes through the opening because they had been unable to contribute money to the monastery.

The chute opening had clearly been tampered with! Fr. Malachi peered at the long, fresh scratches marring the surface of the box. Someone had used an instrument—a crowbar, a hammer, or a screwdriver—to pry open the chute opening. With the aid of a chair or a ladder, a small person could have slipped through the opening into the sacristy and taken those holy cards that were burned on the altar. The sacristy, a small room off the altar area, was always kept locked to all but those who served or prepared the altar, because of the holy artifacts, the gold and silver. Although the Abbot was horrified, he also felt a vague relief. None of the monks were small enough to crawl through the sacristy opening! Well then, who? Fr. Malachi withdrew cotton gloves from his pocket, fully cognizant that he was tampering with the murder scene. He fitted his key into the lock of the sacristy door, and entered.

Inside the sacristy, he was disappointed to find that everything had been dusted, opened, and, in his mind, desecrated. There was no need for him to search. The room had been thoroughly examined, and when he opened the drawer that held the holy cards, he noticed that they had been removed. Fr. Malachi experienced a little frisson of fear and hurried from the sacristy, knowing that he had made the discovery of how someone had gained access to the cards; yet he lacked the skill to discern who had been motivated to enter the chapel, deface the ceiling, and commit murder. He felt like Elijah standing on the mountain before Yahweh when a hurricane occurred, followed by an earthquake, followed by fire. But where was the 'still small voice' discerned by Elijah that would reveal to Malachi *who* had disturbed the peaceful current of their lives at St. Andrew's?

# CHAPTER XIII

*Muses of poetry with lyre never support those in sorrow by any healing remedies, but rather do ever foster the sorrow by poisonous sweets.*

~**Boethius**

Lunch was a strange affair, to say the least, after a morning of murder and widespread suspicion that caused even the most tranquil of the monks to look behind their backs and cross themselves more than usual. The regular services of prayer and chant had been kept, in the administrative hallway, with the chapel closed to worship. But the monks' voices had been tremulous, and their cadence not quite in sync, somehow, even as they followed the sheet music Fr. Paul had prepared only days before.

Fr. Malachi knew that they would have to resume not only their disciplined daily life, but a rigorous practice schedule if they were to be ready for the recording of *Godspeak II* right after Christmas. Advent was no time for commercial business to go on as usual. It wasn't as penitential a time as Lent, the 40 days leading up to Easter. But it was a mirror of Lent in that its scant four weeks, which always included four Sundays, also led up to a major holy festival: the Feast of the Nativity, Christmas.

And now he could hardly focus on his text that morning, it was so painful to look out at the sea of trusting faces and know that he had failed them. Yet he still bore the responsibility of shepherding them all through this valley of the shadow, not to mention keeping his own soul safe in the fold for the duration and beyond.

And now the familiar ritual of sitting down together to break Communion bread, to share the wine, to lift up prayers for life and sustenance, while the poor bodies of two among their number were lying still, their life savagely sucked out—by whom?

Fr. Eli had always been suspicious of even the good brothers around him, thinking someone might be out to poison him, as some monks had once tried to poison St. Benedict's wine in order to remove him as their Abbot. Fr. Eli even broke a glass pitcher in the refectory once, typical of his flamboyant style, to verify that he was a central figure like Benedict, whose own pitcher had broken as he blessed it, thwarting the plot and proving it held poison wine.

The old prophet took precautions. He used to say, "Trust God, but tie up your camel," and would sniff his food and taste his water gingerly for any untoward hint of menace. He drove the cook crazy, Fr. Malachi recalled, smiling, until he remembered Eli was gone, and felt a cold chill down his spine again.

He glanced over at the seat where he and Eli had sat together just days, or was it hours ago? Well, the old man had always spoken in his storybook way about "sitting in Elijah's chair." Now it really *was* empty. He noticed at lunch that none of the other monks chose to go near it.

After the discovery of the jimmied alms door in the sacristy, the Abbot determined to do some more sleuthing on his own before taking his suspicions to Detective Wagner. He saw the reporters hovering around the front gate like vultures seeking a scoop, and being turned back by the (in his opinion) unnecessary guard the police had set near the door.

Apparently the police hadn't come back with the warrants to check monks' rooms yet. Much better to do his own snooping first, before they did. He might be able to eliminate some possibilities, or find some new angles, before that overconfident police detective-woman tried to take over their orderly life, and made a bad situation worse. As if it could BE worse! He corrected himself sardonically.

He was still wondering about Fr. Eli's movements that night. Why would he have been carrying his much-touted "revelations" around at that hour, and what would have caused him to walk over to the rocky shore of the lake? He had never been that fond of water. What had he seen, or thought he saw?

And several people had noted that he uncharacteristically wore a wide, gray wool cape over his red alb strangely chosen for that routine Compline service. Had he scheduled some appointment afterward? Did he see it as a crucial final deliverance of his evidence against the Order?

Malachi chastised himself for having gone to bed early, after his exhausting talk with Fr. Jean that night, and now he had to sort out new confessions from his usually stable, dependable Prior. Often Fr. Malachi himself would have gone in for a pre-dawn prayer time at the very railing where Paul was found. It could have been him, slumped there like an unwilling sacrifice before the altar...

Paul must have stayed on in the chapel practicing. Some of the monks had heard the sounds of the organ after they left the chapel that night. No one knew for sure when the chords ended. Paul must have had a great deal to pray about. Yet Fr. Malachi didn't believe he would have wanted to end his life. And since no weapon was found at the scene, someone else had to have taken it away. Everyone knew that Paul was so enthusiastically invested in his — their — music, for the future. However, the Abbot also realized that Paul was undergoing conflict about his 'fame' and how it fit into the true vocation of a monk. Didn't they all have doubts and fears in their own ways? Surely it was murder, but why, and by whom?

Fr. Malachi had never likened himself to a private investigator; but as he reflected on the job the Bishop had commissioned him with, of finding the murderer, he thought of the investigations he had performed on the psyche when he practiced psychiatry and suddenly felt he shouldn't downplay his skills. The ability to imagine the intent of a murderer, searching for a distorted mind capable of killing, *could* possibly coincide with the analytical skills associated with his former profession.

Fr. Malachi sighed deeply. He'd far rather lose himself in the stillness of contemplation. He remembered the words the contemporary writer Eckhart Tolle had offered regarding the meaning of this life. Tolle had said that the purpose of the world was to make one suffer, to create the suffering that seems to be what a person needs to awaken and become enlightened. Fr. Malachi surmised he was well on his way toward awakening, then, for he hadn't felt such suffering since his wife died.

He turned his attention to the job that the Bishop had given him to do. He'd visit Fr. Eli's cottage and search it thoroughly before the police returned, and if he discovered a piece of evidence there, he wouldn't conceal it from Detective Wagner. However, he knew that he'd find it difficult to implicate the prophet, despite the fact that the manic activities of the old man had disturbed the peace of the monastery. At some level of his thinking, he perceived that peace and hospitality didn't always complement one another.

He'd embrace the moment and the task at hand. Again, he thought of Tolle's concept that the human mind had evolved to a state of noisiness and enlargement of ego, and had reached a point of madness so that violence was rampant in the world. Was that the message Fr. Eli had attempted to convey? Why would anyone murder him for espousing his beliefs, for being enlightened?

Fr. Malachi pushed back his chair and left the refectory, bound for Fr. Eli's cottage. He'd search for the murder weapon, which he tentatively assumed was the ominous-looking katana the prophet had worn on his belt. He couldn't recall whether Fr. Eli had worn the sword when he attended Compline. Perhaps he had left it in his room where a mad man had found it and used it to kill Fr. Paul. And where was Fr. Eli's cane? Did it somehow matter?

Fr. Malachi experienced a strange release as he began his investigation, a return of the old exhilaration he had felt when he probed the psyche looking for the culprit buried in a patient's unconscious mind, coaxing the patient to let a painful memory surface in a confrontation that would inevitably free him from a burdensome past.

◌

He approached the guest cottage where Fr. Eli had been staying through Malachi's own extension of hospitality. It had simply been the right thing, he still felt, to let the old man do his work, as any monk would have the privilege of doing in between other clerical commitments. Fr. Eli did have some credentials. Fr. Malachi had seen his ordination papers from St. Ivan's on the Eastern border of Russia where Eli had lived and served, from the days after his parents were both shot in the Revolution. Those monks had vouched for his identity, and Malachi had no reason to believe the paperwork was fraudulent, but what if it was?

The door pushed open easily. Fr. Eli's bed was rumpled but didn't look recently slept in. A drawer in a bedside table was slightly ajar, but all he saw inside were a broken comb, some frayed pieces of string, a weathered copy of the Bible in Russian, and a grayed handkerchief. The prophet traveled light.

There was his cane, propped up in the corner. Malachi had always suspected that it was more for show than necessity, especially after hearing of Fr. Eli's dance at The Camellia Bar several weeks ago. Had it all started then? November 30, the newspaper had said. The Feast of St. Andrew's. The saint's day that always fell near the first Sunday of Advent. Eli must have skipped the monastery's afternoon celebration, the Feast Day tea and cakes in the refectory, instead choosing to go to a pub? Thinking back, he didn't recall seeing him there, despite the free food. Something was strange about that.

But as Malachi glanced around the small room, at its spartan furnishings, what was most noticeable was an absence: the katana of that famously reported dance was nowhere to be seen. No sheath, no sword. That artifact had been incredibly dear to Fr. Eli. Not quite in keeping with his prophetic look of dingy albs and sometime flamboyant fringed cape, but, then, Fr. Eli's background was an unlikely mix of Benedictine simplicity and ethnic pride. His mother's father, reportedly, had been a Japanese Samurai and had passed the historic sword down to him.

But Eli was also fiercely Eastern European, wary of social change and movements in peoples and societies that might upend the order of things. That is, unless he himself got to be the revolutionary! What unwanted surprise had he been preparing to spring on them, and when?

Fr. Malachi wished he could ask Eli himself, but talking to the dead was not a valid part of his tradition. Should he tell Detective Wagner what he knew? She didn't seem interested in hearing any more about Eli himself after she got wind of the katana. Forensics were everything now.

Malachi believed in motive. Even though the dapper, fictional detective Lord Peter Wimsey was supposed to have said "motives are moonshine. When you know how you know who." Well, the *how* of Paul's death was almost certainly a sword. But the *who* was far from clear.

Malachi felt in his heart that Fr. Eli was innocent of something so cold blooded. But his brandishing of knives and possession of a sword was indisputable. What if the police concluded that he *hadn't* killed Paul but had himself been stoned after an accidental slip? Then the killer really was still loose and alive, possibly still on monastery property.

Following Mass in the improvised chapel of the refectory, Fr. Malachi was surprised by the early appearance of Detective Wagner and Detective Bronson.

"We have warrants to search the rooms of Fr. Eli and Fr. Jean for starters," Detective Wagner told Fr. Malachi as he exited the refectory. She had apparently slept badly, as dark circles underlined her hazel eyes. In the bright morning light, she looked haggard.

"I'm sure that you'll find nothing to implicate these good men, but you're prepared with warrants, I see. I understand your desire to search, but before you assemble any more men from your crime team, may I suggest a thorough search of the place where a lot of activity seems to have occurred?" Fr. Malachi looked into Detective Wagner's inscrutable eyes and hesitated for a moment.

"Such as?"

"Such as the lake."

"My men searched the lakeshore yesterday. There was nothing there except the floating dead body of your so-called prophet, and a few soggy manuscript pages."

Fr. Malachi cleared his throat. "There is the lake itself." He glanced at the calm surface of the water, glittering in the morning sunlight. "At Compline, the evening service before Fr. Paul's unfortunate demise, I don't remember having seen the katana or sword Fr. Eli usually wore on his belt. I asked the other monks if they had recalled seeing it on his person, and they think it wasn't in its usual place on his belt. Perhaps he had removed it. But I strongly suspect the person who found the katana used it to kill Fr. Paul, then threw it into the lake."

"And why would you think that?" Detective Wagner snapped.

"After looking at the fatal wound, I surmised that the instrument might have been a long, keenly sharp knife, perhaps an Oriental sword similar to the one Fr. Eli wore. And the lake would have been a good repository for such a weapon once someone had used it to kill."

Detective Wagner glanced at Fr. Malachi, and the air was briefly filled with a thick silence. Finally, she turned to Detective Bronson and barked an order. "Get the Sheriff's recovery dive team in here. Tell him to send his best emergency divers with full search equipment. We'll need at least three divers. One who'll search for evidence; a second one who can make sure he's safe, and a third one to record any evidence they discover. Tell them to bring their Jack Stay sweep and to alert a forensic expert in the CI lab that something will soon be on its way to him. Tell the Sheriff to send me men who have done at least 10,000 dives."

Having delivered a long order, Detective Wagner seemed to wind down, and the menacing expression on her face disappeared. "Maybe you should take up detective work on the side," she said to Fr. Malachi. "I thought about the sword, of course, but dismissed the possibility of finding it in the lake, thinking it'd turn up in one of the monks' rooms when we searched them. However, I think the lake deserves a good sweep before we proceed to rooms anyway." Detective Wagner seemed to be uncharacteristically flustered and changed the subject. "Do you serve coffee to police workers?"

"We serve a full breakfast in the refectory if you'd like," Fr. Malachi invited her. His own stomach rumbled loudly. "Hospitality is our leitmotif," he added.

"Don't need a field hand breakfast. Can't work when I'm filled with food, and no telling what we'll drag up around here to turn my stomach." Detective Wagner's sarcasm bit into the hospitable invitation.

Fr. Malachi ignored her acerbic remark, wondering if he could snatch a sweet roll if he offered to get the coffee for the two crime detectives. "I'll be glad to get two cups of coffee for you and Detective Bronson." He nodded at her assistant, who was pacing on the walk, delivering orders into his cell phone. "You can rest on the bench while I'm gone." Fr. Malachi looked upward at a few gray clouds that had appeared and were hovering over the lake. "The weather looks restless. I hope the divers don't have to work in a rainstorm."

"It's just typical Louisiana weather. Always threatening," Detective Wagner said. "I'd appreciate the coffee and service. The team should be here within the hour. It's the best dive team in the South. They've had to dive following torrential rains when rivers and streams had extremely strong currents. This job is a piece of cake. They do their training on lakes."

When Fr. Malachi disappeared into the refectory, the detective and her assistant sat down on the stone bench of the walkway, both of them looking out at the lake as if they were waiting for something to suddenly surface and disturb its placid waters.

Thirty minutes later, a van arrived and three divers got out to unload a Jack Stay sweep at the lakeside facing the site of the refectory. Before Detective Wagner could put down her coffee cup, a diver was in the water and had begun to run a search line at the bottom of the water. The line consisted of a rope with a weight on each end. The diver searched along the rope, and when he reached the end, he moved the weight forward. Then he searched back along the rope to the other end and moved that weight forward so that he completed the search twice. The diver had been working fifteen minutes by Detective Wagner's wristwatch when the secondary diver, onshore, started running a tape measure from the primary diver to a large cypress tree near the shore. She knew they had hit pay dirt. They repeated this procedure, measuring to another tree on shore, this time a large live oak tree, thus triangulating a location.

"Well, that was fast work!" Detective Wagner exclaimed. "They've measured the distance from shore to the point where they found something," she explained to Fr. Malachi who stood beside her. "Now, they're filling a container with lake water and will keep the object in the same water it has been in. I can't tell what the object is from here. Whoever disposed of it couldn't throw anything very far or didn't swim out very far to dispose of it."

The primary diver, clad in his seal-like diving suit, swam until he reached the shallow waters, then waded ashore and approached Detective Wagner. In his hands he held a long, water-tight container. "You can see it in the lab, ma'am, but I can tell you that it's a Samurai sword. It has a black composition handle with black cord wrap, black finish metal on the tsuba with gold artwork and a tempered steel blade about two feet long, and it looks squeaky clean. Whoever used it probably wiped it with some of the grasses around here and threw the grasses into the water. That grass is probably washed clean by now, if you could find it."

"Good job! Your name, sir?"

"Forrest Cooper, ma'am. Do you want us to search further?"

"You can sweep all around the perimeter of the lake, but I think we've probably uncovered all that we're going to find in the water." Detective Wagner smiled at the diver and flashed a V sign at Fr. Malachi. He gave her a concise smile and walked away from the scene, feeling as confused as he had been the morning he first discovered the pile of ashes on the altar, so long ago now, it seemed.

# CHAPTER XIV

*We are thirsty fish in His blissful water, like the starving buried in the feast of His sustenance.*

*≈* **R u m i**

Fr. Jean looked out at his fellow monks from the improvised choir stall. His prominent position in the front row, in Fr. Paul's usual singing position, solidified the painful realization that *he himself* was now both choirmaster *and* cantor for The Heavenly Choir. In the processional he had felt he was dream-walking, dream-singing.

The necessity of a joint funeral for the two slain monks had brought the Order to such an emotional pitch that he was sure the others were probably also performing as usual, but in shock mode: Everyone seemed to be experiencing a sense of unreality, mixed in with fear and guilt, however false and toxic, at least in his case. Fr. Jean had already confessed his feelings about Fr. Paul; and he would never have harmed Paul or anyone physically. But would the police believe that?

Fr. Malachi would have his hands full with counseling once they all got through this essential rite of consecrating these two troubled souls and respectfully entombing their bodies in the wall crypt, exterior to the monastery. Interment *above* ground rather than *below* ground, as it would have been in a region of higher elevation, was standard in lower Louisiana. Though Fr. Jean, a transplant to this region, was accustomed to the departed ones resting apart from the monastery's walls, this amounted to another symbolic level of estrangement. Was he, Fr. Jean, somehow partly responsible for these losses at some level he couldn't comprehend in order to make amends for?

Fr. Jean's resonant tenor voice rang out within the refectory with the musical confidence that came from rigorous voice training and sincere dedication to this *liturgy*, this 'work of the people' of which chant was an essential element. People passed on, monastic orders themselves shifted, but this music of the soul endured through the generations, steady voices praising God in continuous song that somehow held things together, even through tragedy.

Fr. Malachi, intoning the lines of the Requiem Mass also in chant, as was their tradition, looked stalwart and resigned. But Fr. Jean knew that he too was reeling from the horrendous events of the past few days, and the implication that someone among them might at least be complicit with a murderer. Getting through the burial service, this important consecration of 'ashes to ashes,' was a necessary rite of passage into what would come next. But its consolations were few.

Soon they would sing the *Dies Irae,* the 13th-century Latin hymn that described the Day of Judgment, the Last Trump sounding, summoning souls to appear before the Throne of God.

> *Libera me, Domine, de morte aeterna, in die illa tremenda:*
> *Quando caeli movendi sunt et terra*
> *Dum veneris judicare saeculum per ignem.*

> Deliver me, O Lord, from eternal death on that fearful day,
> when the heavens and the earth are moved,
> when you come to judge the world with fire.

Fr. Jean was quaking within himself as he nevertheless clearly and steadily sang out the Introit, its Latin phrasing known to all as the blessing:

> Eternal rest grant unto them, O Lord,
> and let perpetual light shine upon them.

He knew well the fearful imagery that would soon be rising up around them in the *Dies Irae,* or 'day of wrath' segment. The effect was always more accusing than consoling. Where was the hope, the promise of elusive peace that was supposed to come to them through their mutual dedication to prayer and work, all amid companionable brotherly love? The extreme terms of the burial liturgy seemed to mock their feeble attempts to sustain a life of the soul here in this sacred place. Evil was undeniable in its phrases and predicted effects: "I am made to tremble and I fear, because of the judgment that will come, and also the coming wrath. When the heavens and the earth are moved that day... day of wrath, calamity, and misery, day of great and exceeding bitterness."

Fr. Jean tried to clear his mind of these thoughts. The two silent bodies in their plain pine coffins would later be taken to the marble wall mausoleum for a graveside service of greater simplicity and calm. He had to pull himself together for all of these rites, or his own demeanor would give away the doubts and turmoil he still felt inside.

❧

John Landry had managed to disassociate himself from his underlying sorrowful feelings during the funeral at St. Andrew's by sitting in a hard, metal folding chair at the back of the refectory, where he refrained from glancing up at the improvised altar and the caskets of the dead monks, especially the coffin enclosing his beloved star cantor, Fr. Paul. He had diverted himself by keeping his eyes fixed on the large murals lining the walls of the refectory. The Dutch artist, Vroon, had certainly made St. Andrew's Monastery famous long before *Godspeak* had appeared. But the paintings were an added enhancement for CD sales, as people came to view Vroon's magnificent paintings. And when their tour of the artwork ended, they walked over to the gift shop where the CDs were prominently displayed and promoted by docents.

The morning following the funeral, Landry stood before his nine-foot pier mirror, a legacy from his grandiose mother, and regarded his own reflection in the long glass. He had selected a conservative, navy blue serge suit and an aquamarine-colored silk tie for the interview scheduled with Fr. Jean. Perfect, he thought. He went to the small, mahogany spinet desk in his bedroom and picked up the new contract he'd present to Fr. Jean, then removed two folded sheets of paper from one of the cubbyholes in the desk. The day Fr. Paul had banished him with those insulting words about his sexual orientation, he had returned to the Abbey during Compline while the monks were at prayer and snooped in the star cantor's room. To his chagrin, he had discovered a shocking to-do list within the pages of a lone illustrated volume of *Lives of the Saints* where he knew Fr. Paul kept his newest alternative chants. It read:

1. Deal with Jean
2. Get rid of Landry
3. Take over publicity from Fr. Malachi

The list had inflamed him further and, feeling intensely spiteful, he removed the list and the composition sheet on which Fr. Paul had written his latest chant. Today, he felt a twinge of guilt about stealing the sheets of paper from Fr. Paul's room and because *he had felt relief* when he learned that Fr. Paul had died and wouldn't be able to carry out the intentions of that list. Landry no longer had any use for the papers he had discovered in Fr. Paul's room, but he was paranoid about police searches, and what if they found the list and the musical page in his desk? Then he'd become even more of a suspect! He unfolded and flattened the papers, read the shocking list again, then refolded both sheets in neat squares before putting them into his inner coat pocket. Landry decided he would go about this CD contract business like killing snakes—carefully. He examined himself in the mirror and appraised his appearance as highly presentable, perhaps even attractive enough to gain Fr. Jean's favor.

On the way to the monastery, Landry again crossed the small bridge where the melancholy Mrs. Green had stood, and felt a strange nostalgia overtake him. He loved his small world and hoped he'd be able to keep the overpriced home that he had bought in Mill Pond when *Godspeak* had become an overwhelming sensation. He didn't want to live near Lake Ponchartrain because of the threat of hurricanes, and the thought of living in any of the so-called redneck villages in other areas of Louisiana made him cringe. The redneck view about gay men was appalling, actually dangerous, and he thanked God for the French influence in his part of the world, where he enjoyed the fact that a more embracing view of human sexuality prevailed.

Landry speculated about Fr. Jean's position as choirmaster. He had a beautiful, haunting voice, but it lacked the volume of Fr. Paul's voice. However, he was sure that the former success of the choir was intact, and substituting a new voice might create an even bigger stir. Fr. Jean was certainly handsome enough! And, actually, the murders seemed to have created a major jump in sales during the past few days. The funeral services had attracted a large crowd, and immediately following the last prayers, an overflow of people had hastened to the gift shop to snatch up copies of the last CD featuring Fr. Paul. Everything was working out, despite the horrific murders.

As Landry drove into the parking lot of the monastery, he glimpsed Fr. Jean sitting in a lawn chair beside the winter garden of cabbage plants. Curious place for prayer, he thought. Fr. Jean seemed to be contemplating the great heads of cabbage while his hands slowly moved the black beads of his rosary.

Landry regarded the monk dubiously. He wondered if Fr. Jean was reciting some kind of penance for dark deeds he had committed. He held onto some suspicion that the new cantor might actually have murdered Fr. Paul so that he could emerge in the limelight.

"Composing a chant to cabbages?" Landry asked playfully as he approached Fr. Jean.

Fr. Jean smiled. "Seemed like a good place to ponder all that has happened in the last few days. You know, Cato the Elder once praised the cabbage for its medicinal qualities. I've heard that you can make a paste from its leaves and cure acute inflammation by smearing it on the inflamed spot."

"I'd hope that the paste could help inflammations of the heart that are symptomatic of sadness," Landry said. He remained standing and wondered if the cabbage patch would be the scene of the contract signing.

"Did you see Fr. Paul after he sent you away the other day?" Fr. Jean suddenly asked. He stopped moving the rosary beads and looked intently at the publicist.

"I'm afraid that's my last memory of Paul. Do you think I'm capable of murder, Jean?"

"I think that the murders we commit in that inflamed heart you mentioned are possible for anyone, and sometimes people act on vengeful impulses."

"Though you probably won't believe me, I really cared about Fr. Paul. We developed this venture together. Who would have guessed that the whole world would fall in love with a frickin' *medieval* art form? Fr. Paul was the face, the voice of The Heavenly Choir. The genius behind the success of *Godspeak*, the renowned reviver of Chant for modern ears!" He blushed and felt his own voice quavering in spite of himself. "Besides," he added, "I wouldn't be so stupid as to get rid of such a rich source of income." Landry put his hand under his chin as though thinking his next point through. "I could accuse *you* of envying his popularity to the point of murder. But of course everyone knows that you're a man of benign nature." Landry caressed his silk tie absentmindedly.

Fr. Jean ignored the accusation that had become a sarcastic compliment. He stood up and overturned the lawn chair. "We can go into the library for the signing. Fr. Malachi needs to witness this agreement."

"And there is one more thing." Landry gave Fr. Jean his most conspiratorial half-gaze that never failed to put other people on edge and force them to listen to his pontifications. "I actually think I know who should be the main suspect. And he's a little guy, well, like me, but did you know there is someone right here in the Abbey who has murdered before? And Fr. Malachi, well, he must have his reasons for not warning the rest of you. If it was me, though... " He smiled snarkily. "I'm just saying. Watch your back."

Fr. Jean tried to dismiss any consideration of these low-level insinuations of the always-gossipy publicist. Yet these were extremely dire issues, and he wondered how this outsider thought he knew something about a monk that Fr. Malachi had never told his own. This was preposterous.

"We're here for a contract signing," Fr. Jean said soberly. "Let's proceed." He began walking slightly ahead of Landry.

"I'm ready. Sorry I accused you. I know you're a good man, and I also think your voice will enhance the sales of *Godspeak*." Landry became obsequious. "I'm ready to do everything I can to publicize your talent." He reached for Fr. Jean's arm in a conciliatory manner, but the monk pulled back instinctively. The gentle Haitian was repulsed by this self-satisfied, slick promoter and his superficial camaraderie. But he himself would choose to do what was best for the Order. He would sign the contract, and he'd humbly take over the popular former cantor's work. Rather than bringing a sense of glory or gain, it would feel like a form of penitence for the ill-will between him and Fr. Paul in these last months. He'd offer it up.

Fr. Jean knew in his heart that God had forgiven him. But would the police, using their typical attempts to attribute motive, target him in this investigation, since he was clearly the one who had the most to gain? Except maybe for Landry, if he had committed murder as retribution for being spurned.

Fr. Jean bowed his head. The lengths some people will go to to ensure their own prosperity, he thought ruefully. Yes, the lengths. Was it possible Landry had really acted on his resentment of Paul's condemnation of him? The man was no Aelred, that was certain. His crass manner and flashy style of dress were repugnant to Fr. Jean. Landry even acted as though, despite their mutual suspicions, he could now assume an immediate intimacy of sorts with his new cantor! Fr. Jean shivered with distaste. The little publicist didn't know the meaning of spiritual friendship and hadn't even pretended to want a relationship with Paul that had any deeper dimension.

"I'm not very good at singing pop music," he said aloud, "but if it benefits the children in Haiti, I'll commit myself to learning how to compose alternative chant. I understand that even the nuns now are performing this kind of music. Paul was working toward radio time, using a broader repertoire. But you must learn to shield our community better. Our object with the music is to inspire faith in those people who have moved away from the Church."

"A lofty goal, along with the one to acquire millions of dollars to send to Haiti. You'll feel more comfortable with alternative chant if you practice it daily. Do you think the Abbot is in his office?" Landry, satisfied with the preliminaries to their joint venture, had become impatient. He began walking toward the administration building, and Fr. Jean, again busy with his rosary beads, slowly followed behind, looking pale and somber.

# CHAPTER XV

*People think that sights, sounds, and touch from the outside world constitute reality. But the brain constructs what it perceives on past experience.*

*⟶* **Stephen M. Kosslyn**

*C*otille hurried along the dirt path through the woods along the river toward her cottage. It was First Dark, and she wanted to reach home before darkness overtook her—or worse still, before getting caught in the dense mists that often rolled in and hung in the woods. Big Branch Marsh in Lacombe wasn't far away, and she knew that some people had sighted the dreaded *loup-garou* ghost in the wilderness swamp at night. The moon had risen above the trees, and the air in the woods was cold, a sharp scent of pine trees lingering everywhere. The drawn-out hoot of an owl startled her, and she thought about how her Cajun mother had warned her that such a long hoot announced death. Well, it was too late for that. Two deaths had already happened. Cotille shuddered, terrified that she would be captured by a werewolf. Thank god, she wasn't carrying a child. At times, she recalled from her mother's warnings, the *loup-garou* would kill a woman carrying an infant on the way through the woods toward home so he could give the child to a she-wolf to nurture. She quickened her pace until she was almost running, branches snapping underfoot, shadows and sudden noises increasing her fright. She thought she heard a mysterious grunting coming from a clump of underbrush and imagined a form with a werewolf head lurking there, waiting to suck the blood from her body by means of its large fangs and serrated teeth.

Cotille screamed when a figure with a wolf head jumped out at her and grasped her arm. Her screaming ceased when she heard a child laughing and saw the small form tear a wolf-head mask from its head.

102

"Gotcha!" he jeered. "Gotcha, old woman. You thought I was the wolf man, didn't you?"

Cotille swatted at the small form of her nephew, Claude, then pulled him into her arms as if she should comfort him rather than herself. Claude was a thin, elfin-faced boy, his ears as pointed as the devil's own, his hair sticking up in a buzz cut, and his lips risible in their width and fullness. He was an unattractive, dark-eyed child, almost bizarre-looking, and Cotille knew he loved mischief—malicious mischief.

"I scared you, didn't I?" Claude said gleefully. "How'd you like my red eyes?"

"Hush, Claude. There may be a real *loup-garou* lurking about. The moon is full, and some say Marie Lauveau, the Voodoo Queen, is still alive as a werewolf and living near Lake Pontchartrain."

Cotille clasped her nephew's grotesquely large hand and pulled him along, anxious to be in her single-room cottage near the river.

"Stop hurrying me," Claude protested. "There's nothing to hurry for."

"I'll let you play with the holy cards," Cotille offered. "It's getting colder, and we'll be warm at home. You can sleep downstairs with me instead of going up to the *garconniere*."

Claude grinned and began to match her pace, and within minutes they had reached a small cypress cabin with a narrow porch and outside stairs leading up to an attic bedroom Cotille had called the *garconniere*. The chimney of the cabin, made of mud and moss, was whitewashed to protect it from the elements. Cotille had no idea how long the structure had been there, but it was her property, and developers hadn't been able to budge her from it when they bought land around her and constructed the expensive homes in Mill Pond Subdivision. She had shown them who really belonged in the good sites along the river!

Inside the cabin, she lit a kerosene lamp and placed it on the hand-turned cypress table, pulling up a sturdy chair with stretched rawhide seat. From the top of the rough-hewn table, she took a small bag and removed two bleached white bones from the wings of a chicken. With needle and black thread, she tied the two wings together in an equal-armed cross, chanting: "The crossbones will hold negativity/into your bone marrow it will go/evil and negative energy."

"What are you doing, Aunt Cotille?" Claude asked. He put down the cards illustrated with pictures of Jesus, Mary, and other saints, watching as Cotille put her hand in a basin on the table, cupped some water, and sprinkled it over the bone amulet. After she had doused the amulet with water, she shook salt over the strange cross, finally passing the amulet through the flame of a black candle she had lit. She had also lit a small burner of incense and waved the amulet over it, chanting an affirmation of negative energy. After letting the amulet cool, she attached it to a long black string and slipped it around her neck.

"There," she said to Claude. "That will work as good as the Evil Eye."

Claude blinked at her warily. Could some spell help protect him from the eyes of the other Small One? He wouldn't tell his aunt the danger of the one who spied at odd hours and listened to words that drifted through the night air, just as Claude himself had learned to do, pilfering other people's secrets and storing them up to spring like traps when the time was ripe. Claude returned to shuffling his cards, and Cotille picked up a rag-tag patchwork quilt lying over one of the chairs at the kitchen table. She began to sew into the quilt another large square of gray wool, a material not unlike that of the texture of the cloak Fr. Eli had once worn.

ℭℜ

Following the search and discovery of the Samurai sword by the dive team, Detective Wagner had received a call on her cell to return to the police station. There, she worked steadily on another case until nightfall, then went to her apartment and telephoned an old friend to come over and share a bottle of Chardonnay with her. She had clicked off the lamp on her bedside table at exactly 2:00 a.m., tossed in bed uneasily for several hours, and finally kicked back the blue "baby doll" quilt on her bed at 5:30 a.m., eager to get back to the investigation at the monastery. She left her apartment without a drop of her customary dark-roast coffee and picked up Detective Bronson at 6:30, knowing she was heavy-lidded and slightly irascible.

"Pretty soon, they're going to start proselytizing me," she quipped to her assistant on the drive to St. Andrew's. "I always arrive right after Mass, but they'll want me to come in and chant with them if we continue these early morning visits."

"Maybe it wouldn't hurt to have the help of some Higher Power," Detective Bronson muttered somewhat sheepishly.

His boss ignored him, rolling her eyes. She held up her palms, counting on the fingers of her right hand. "The logical thing would be that the old prophet-manque did it with his own sword to protect the community from forsaking its ancient musical traditions." Detective Wagner couldn't keep the cynicism out of her voice. To her the monks were like children who had up to now enjoyed the protection of the clerical 'nursery,' unscathed by the realities of the world she lived in daily. She paused, then counted on the second finger: "But then, who retaliated and killed *him*?"

"We keep turning up evidence that doesn't point us decisively toward anyone," Detective Bronson said. "Fr. Eli's cottage was unlocked, so anyone could have taken that sword. He might have died trying to get it back..."

"But he wrote a treatise accusing his fellow monks. Lots of smoldering accusations he hadn't yet acted on. I don't understand half of it, but the pages practically steamed with rancor, couched in gobbledygook phrases. Even the blurred lines of script looked as though he'd had poison in his pen."

"Do we need to decipher it all?"

"I've got someone on that, sifting through some stuck-together pages. Doubt they'll turn up much. It didn't exactly sound like a how-to-murder manual or a list of missed opportunities to slice and dice a set of clerical vocal cords..."

"Murder happens fast, but collecting evidence is slow." He glanced at the back seat, which was loaded with plastic bags, cardboard boxes, evidence tags, rubber gloves, everything a well-equipped collection kit should hold. "You reckon the murderer just walks by us every time we go out to the monastery?"

"Well, it wouldn't be the first time a murderer circled us for awhile. I'm really stumped. The most likely suspects who remain, excluding Fr. Eli who seems to have been marked as a victim, are Fr. Jean and those two lovebird monks. But you know, we haven't combed the area for other suspects, so we could be barking up the wrong tree."

"Don't forget that flashy dresser, the publicist," Detective Bronson reminded her.

"Oh yes, he danced around us fairly well at the last interrogation. His MO is 'faint and fall out,' like some Victorian virgin. It's clear that Fr. Paul meant more to him than a cash cow. Maybe we'll find something specific on him to inspire a second questioning. Let's not let him get far out of sight." Detective Wagner pressed a well-manicured hand to her forehead and yawned. "I have sleep deprivation in the worst way," she said.

"It's the nature of this beast, detective work. And since when did you start requiring sleep?"

"Since I acquired a night visitor, which is none of your business."

Detective Bronson, surprised at the idea of her having a swain and that she would confess it, looked at her normally stony profile and decided not to rush in where angels feared to tread. He wondered if there really was such a night visitor or if she had confessed this because most of the police force thought she was frigid and incapable of arousing desire in a man. He knew she wouldn't volunteer a name or the profession of this mysterious person until she was ready. Already, she had returned to her shell by the time she finished speaking.

"Whose room first?" she asked, ignoring Detective Bronson's searching look. "How about the new choirmaster's digs?"

"Well, he did inherit a coveted position. And he looks like he's ready to implode any moment."

"The word is explode."

"No, the word is implode... like collapse inside," Detective Bronson argued.

Detective Wagner ignored him, swerved into the driveway of the monastery, and backed into a parking space near the entrance to the administration building. As they entered the building, Fr. Malachi came out of the refectory where Morning Mass had just ended.

"Will you join us for coffee?" he invited.

"We need to get into Fr. Jean's room, then Fr. Eli's cottage," Detective Wagner said tersely.

"Of course, whatever we can do to assist you in this search. However, I assure you..."

"Never mind, Father. I know that you think the inhabitants of this hallowed place are like innocent angels, but someone around here has bad impulse control, if you want to soften the way you say someone murdered two people."

The detectives followed Fr. Malachi into his office and received a key to the choirmaster's room, leaving without further exchange. Fr. Malachi sat down at his desk, covered his face with his hands, and assumed his meditations. He knew he should tell the police about the desecrations that had occurred at the beginning of Advent, the ashes on the altar and the ruined ceiling. These crass acts weren't the first evidences of destruction the Abbey had seen in its history. The entrance of *someone* into the locked sacristy through the alms door was surely significant.

As he saw it, someone had gone to pains to steal the Jesus cards as an initial announcement of this whole assault on the peace of the Order. What if there was satanic activity going on within the wider sphere of this holy place, concurrent with their solemn prayers and oblations, an evil that was poised to attack again soon?

Cʒ

Fr. Jean's room, like all the rooms in the monks' quarters, was austere. It contained a narrow bed, a cypress desk, one hardback chair, a few bookshelves, and the ubiquitous crucifix. Detective Wagner gave the room a cursory glance and began searching the bookshelves.

"What have we here?" Detective Bronson asked. He held up a small leather jacket he had found on a shelf behind vestments in the closet.

"I hope that boy's jacket isn't evidence of something going on that I think is nearly as bad as murder," Detective Wagner said. She eyed the jacket with disgust. "Something like the rampant pedophilia going on in the Roman Catholic churches, maybe. Look in the pockets."

Detective Bronson rummaged in the pockets of the wrinkled jacket and withdrew broken pieces of clay that he laid out and pieced together on the surface of the monk's desk. "Some kind of voodoo doll. I recognize it from past work I did uncovering a group of Cajuns practicing Santeria down in Catahoula Bridge. I'd say this is an object someone used to 'cross' an unsuspecting victim. Has Fr. Jean been teaching voodoo to a young person?"

"I think we need to question our new choirmaster about this,"

Detective Wagner said. She stopped talking abruptly when she heard footsteps approaching, and Fr. Jean appeared in the doorway of his room.

Detective Wagner held up the jacket and spoke one word. "Explain."

Fr. Jean matched her for brevity. "Easily."

"Well..."

"I found this the other day in the farm shed where the monastery tractor is kept," he said. "I'm sorry I didn't volunteer it as evidence but I really didn't feel that it had any bearing on the murder."

"You thought? It appears that all of you in this close-knit brotherhood think no evidence, no person, no-thing bears on the murders committed here. Have you ever heard of withholding evidence?"

"I thought this was just something a child was experimenting with."

"And?"

"And I meant to take it up with Fr. Malachi, who has such strong opposition to voodoo, but so many terrible things have happened here recently, the truth is that I completely forgot about it. I certainly wasn't trying to hide anything."

Fr. Jean made the admission calmly and with such believable probity, Detective Wagner turned her back on him and beckoned Detective Bronson to follow her. Fr. Jean thought that Detective Wagner was experiencing what southerners say when they use the vernacular to define getting angry: She's having a hissy fit. He withdrew his rosary from his pants pocket and began fingering it again.

⟪⟫

As Fr. Malachi sat, pondering how, at the Bishop's directive, he could discover and expose a murderer, he was interrupted in his reverie by the appearance of Sean and Peter.

"May we come in?" Sean asked. Peter stood behind him, obviously reluctant to be exposed to the Abbot's scrutiny. But he followed Sean into the office when Fr. Malachi told them to enter.

"Sit down, brothers. Should I call Cotille for coffee? I'm sure she's hovering somewhere close by."

"She's next door polishing the floor," Sean volunteered, "but we've breakfasted and had our quota of caffeine."

Fr. Malachi looked closely at the two young monks, scrutinizing Peter's sullen face, noticing the palpable tension between the pair. He had expected to have to admonish them about too much closeness after the Bishop's warning and threat to expel them. But he saw that the counseling needed would require a more sensitive touch and encouragement rather than censure. He had perceived in this pair a youthful optimism that gave him hope for the continuation of the Order along the lines of greater depth and understanding of *true love and brotherhood.* Now, not surprisingly, the unbearable tension they all suffered under was eating away at even the pure in heart.

"You seem upset, but, then, we all are," the Abbot said gently. "I've been thinking of summoning the brothers for counsel, and here you are, at least two of our youngest, ready to express their opinions, perhaps?"

"He thinks I'm capable of murder," Peter blurted out. "I trusted that he had forgiven my past, but these murders have made him suspicious of me." Peter's face reddened, and a muscle in his cheek flickered as his jaw tightened.

"Sit down, Peter, and take some deep breaths. You are overwrought. This is a safe place. Remember the Rule, 'Do everything with counsel and you will not be sorry afterward,'" the Abbot said.

"I prefer to stand while speaking," Peter said stiffly. "I became angry when I heard that the Bishop wants the proceeds from our CD to bail out priests who have molested children, and when I talked to Sean about it, I broke the string on my rosary and pulled it apart in his presence. I think he was shocked, but I didn't strike anyone. Sean says that the police have informed you about my past record, which was expunged, I might add. He insisted that we come to you because the trust we have had in our friendship is eroding. He's aware that we don't have a shallow relationship based on selfish desires, but he has become suspicious of me and insinuated that I could have committed murder. He's being unfair." Peter made his accusation against his former soul-mate petulantly and remained standing truculently before the Abbot.

"I can understand your anger, given your history of being molested," the Abbot said carefully, "but why would you desecrate a rosary?" Fr. Malachi remembered the ashes on the altar and the defaced angel in the ceiling of the chapel and pushed the invading suspicions away. These two monks were the ones who had found the ruined Juilliard display too. But why would they be involved?

"I admit I lost control, but I'm not a murderer," Peter protested. "I held my tongue. 'In a flood of words you will not avoid sin,'" he quoted from Chapter 6 of the Rule. "I do believe that the tongue holds the key to life and death, as the Rule also says."

The Abbot turned to Sean. "And why should you suddenly develop these suspicions and antipathy toward your friend?"

Sean glanced at his former admirer who had pledged that they be of one heart and one mind and put his hands over his eyes, rubbing them hard, then opening them wider. "It's too much, too much," he said. "We came here to achieve peace, to be free of fear and offense, and dead bodies turn up in every corner of this place. I really don't think Peter's capable of murder. But when I accused him, I felt my accusation might move him to seek counsel for the anger he has been harboring for years. He needs spiritual direction."

"A rather rude and roundabout way of urging him to seek counsel," the Abbot said disapprovingly. "You need to probe the mind of Aelred a bit deeper. 'Between us there was nothing fake or phony, no immature flirting, no hardness of heart, no beating around the bush, no sneaking,'" the Abbot quoted. "I suggest that you find the time to contemplate those writings more deeply..." The Abbot dismissed Sean with a wave of his hand and his usual blessing, and the chastened monk left his office without protest.

"Now," the Abbot said to Peter. "Now I'll hear your confession, your full confession, and we'll begin to work on this thing called an 'anger issue.' And take your time. I had rather bring my monks to a condition of peace this very day than worry about what the world thinks of us." Fr. Malachi straightened his tall body in the desk chair, his benevolent eyes seeking those of the agonized monk before him. He kept in mind the self-defense killing that had occurred in Peter's past. But surely he was not now eye to eye with a brutal murderer?

◌◌

After Peter departed, Fr. Malachi reluctantly returned his attention to his investigative work. He knew that the police suspected Fr. Jean of an 'envy killing.' But he believed so strongly in his Prior's innocence, he felt compelled to keep to himself the information he had found in Jean's room—the note from Paul threatening to expose Jean's clandestine meeting with Cotille. He recalled his earlier suspicions about Jean, how he could have met Paul in the chapel the night of the murder after all. But, the Abbot reasoned, he and Jean had been up very late talking, and Jean would have been forced to have a surreptitious meeting at almost midnight following their conversation. For some intuitive reason, he didn't believe Jean had returned to the chapel. The note of Fr. Paul asking Fr. Jean to meet him was, apparently, never delivered. That had to be the case, since Fr. Malachi had found it himself, where it lay folded up on Fr. Paul's desk.

Jean was a gentle man, but he had developed considerable moral strength after joining their Order. Fr. Malachi opened his bottom desk drawer where he had placed the threatening note Paul had written and turned to his bookshelves. Opening a copy of Aelred's famous treatise, *Spiritual Friendship*, he slipped the note between two pages and closed it firmly against the possible scrutiny of police intruders.

Fr. Malachi knew his monks, and he believed that Jean would have shrugged off any blatant blackmail attempt Paul might have made. He sighed and decided to take a walk. When spring arrived, he'd resume gardening again; the physical activity always helped him think more clearly. Meanwhile, he'd just walk off the confusion he had been experiencing during the last few days. The Bishop had commanded him to find the murderer, and he was confident the Holy Spirit would provide the guidance, that the clues he needed to solve the spiritual problems were even now hovering over the monastery.

He also paused to examine his own motives. Of course, he would prefer to protect the Order from all this invasive probing. But he couldn't obstruct justice. If only he could have a little more time to sort things out, to identify the culprit himself.

He stepped outdoors, and his spirits lifted, approached soaring, when he saw the police car with the two detectives in the front seat leave the parking lot in a noisy exit. Tires screeched as Detective Wagner applied her 'hissy fit' to the accelerator of the aged black automobile.

The dull gray mist that swirled around St. Andrew's reminded the Abbot of how much he disliked winter and the lack of light that prevailed in warmer months and, to him, increased the radiance of life at the Abbey. He reached the cemetery plot, located just past the perimeters of the lake, on which stood the huge crypts that held former abbots and monks who had joined the saints after leading a sanctified life at St. Andrew's. The huge stone edifices housing several coffins were aboveground due to the unusually high water table underground and bore six or more names on the stone commemorating the departed. However, the crypt appeared large enough to hold only two or three coffins. Fr. Malachi knew that to allow space for more, after a year and a day, the crypt was opened so that an old coffin and the body could be broken up and the remains stored in a lower crypt. Within the oven of the crypt, the Louisiana heat baked those remains as if cremating them, and little was left of any of the bodies. Fr. Malachi smiled ruefully to himself. The Church frowned on cremating bodies for burials, but in the tropical Louisiana climate, the process took place anyway.

He stooped to pick up a fragment of paper that the wind had blown against the wrought iron fence surrounding the crypt. His heart accelerated as he recognized the nearly inscrutable scrawl of Fr. Eli, the foreboding words invading his consciousness: "Desecration and abomination everywhere. Evil eye, glance of malice. Mark 7:22-28: projected from heart of men... defiles men — envy, jealousy, and possessiveness..."

ॐ

He remembered once, while they were sitting in the refectory, Fr. Eli had seemed to point out the window toward the crypt, muttering something about the "abomination of desecration." It was a phrase traditionally applied to a historic event nearly two hundred years before Christ, when the Seleucid conqueror Antiochus IV had marched to Jerusalem, dedicated the holy Jewish temple to Zeus, and erected an image of the pagan god in his own likeness on the high altar. Some even said he had sacrificed a pig in further desecration.

Fr. Malachi pocketed the fragment and thought to himself, *now Fr. Eli's own body was entombed in this 'city of the dead' he had seemed to fear* (as the aboveground complex of tombs was often called). *Ah well, we're all simultaneously saints and sinners: simul iustus et peccator.*

The Abbot, heart pounding, opened the gate in the fence. From his waist where he kept all the keys to his 'kingdom,' he selected one and unlocked the door to the crypt, opening it wide to let in the gray light of the outdoors. Inside the stone house, he found a small white candle in a holder and a box of kitchen matches on a ledge by the door. He lit the candle and took it in hand. As he peered at the huge coffins in the center of the crypt, he gasped at the sight of a large circle of dried blood smeared over the top of one of the two coffins. Inside the circle of dried blood was a large bone, similar to the rib of an animal. A faint rustle startled him, and he glimpsed a huge rat scurrying into a dark corner of the crypt where an extension ladder lay. Beside it were a clay doll, a large black candle, and a holy card. Fr. Malachi stooped and picked up the card, which bore an illuminated facsimile of St. Jude, apostle and martyr.

Fr. Malachi dropped to his knees, touching his forehead and saying, "*Au nom du pere*" (In the name of the Father), touched his breastbone, intoning "*le fils*" (the Son), then his left shoulder, saying "*le Saint Esprit*" (the Holy Spirit), and finally touched his right shoulder, saying, "*Si soit il*" (So be it).

Putting his palms together, he recited from Psalm 51: "Create in me a clean heart, O God; and renew a steadfast spirit within me. Cast me not away from Thy presence, and take not thy Holy Spirit from me. Restore to us the joy of thy salvation, and uphold us with a willing spirit." He stood and gingerly picked up the bone, candle, doll, and the holy card, knowing that he had possibly discovered valuable evidence necessary to solve both the *who* and the *why* of the murders. He felt no satisfaction in the discovery, having to admit that secret voodoo rites had been enacted within the sacred crypt. Judging from the scrap of paper that had blown into his path, Fr. Eli had also made this discovery before he was killed.

Voodoo! The fascination with this superstitious practice remained in his province, even if it had been watered down with rituals mixed with the rites of his Holy Church. Fr. Malachi abhorred the spells and sorcery associated with this ancient practice and felt nauseated as he departed the crypt, holding the objects that some conjurer had used to tap into what amounted, in his opinion, to satanism. He went out the gate and latched it, hurrying back to his office where he could contemplate his findings privately.

# CHAPTER XVI

*The one principle of hell is: "I am my own."*
≈ George MacDonald

Fr. Malachi felt as though he were choking with grief and anguish. He instinctively fingered the bulky ring on his right hand for comfort, feeling the grooves of the gold coin that formed its face, *the face of his Lord,* at least as drawn from the art of some master engraver's imagination.

The ring had been specially made for him by his wife Virginia when he received his M. D. and before he interned for psychiatry so many years ago. The 'Jesus coins,' as they were called, were rare, thousand-year-old coins found in an archaeological dig in a portion of the Holy Land that had been predominantly Muslim at the time. Researchers believed they had been used in commerce by Christians as a kind of 'witness' to their faith. There were 58 in total—and the story of how one of them had come up for sale at Sotheby's and been snagged by his wife at auction was a testimony to the privilege and position she had always enjoyed—and perhaps exploited. But Fr. Malachi felt too much repressed guilt to dwell on its provenance now, as he needed a sure thing to cling to. The hard familiarity of the bulky symbol engracing the fourth finger of his right hand would have to do.

*Jesus, the Messiah, the Victor,* the inscription on the ring read in Greek. And it was to his victorious Lord that Fr. Malachi prayed from the depth of his being, as he sought a way through the labyrinth that life had suddenly become. Where must his true loyalties lie? He had committed his life and soul to God, to the intractable, immutable 'Word,' as Jesus was sometimes called. And specifically to the wisdom of the 9000-word Benedictine Rule that guided the life of the Order.

He felt protective toward his monks, just as he had toward his former psychiatric patients. He'd have to find a way that didn't sell them out or violate his own conscience, that wouldn't imperil his soul. The face on the coin was the One to whom his life belonged, not to himself. "You are not your own. You are bought with a price," as the Apostle Paul said to the Corinthians. A payment of blood. But for what had Fr. Paul's bloody death paid? If he knew the answer to that, he'd be able to identify the murderer, or murderers. And it couldn't happen too soon. *Hear my plea, O Lord!*

Fr. Malachi realized that he had accumulated a formidable collection of evidence he should now pass on to Detective Wagner, but he was reluctant to share it with her for fear she'd attack Jean. After all, Jean was the monk who had met with Cotille about voodoo activity, and much of the data he held was related to voodoo, even the holy cards that had been stolen, for some voodooienes used them to implore various saints to assist them in their work. He had no confidence in the police and preferred to do his own sleuthing; but he now had discovered so much, at this point of the investigation he might be accused of withholding. He must call Detective Wagner, he conceded to himself.

Fr. Malachi disliked calling Detective Wagner while she worked at the station, as the detective made caustic remarks about the murders in a loud voice, proclaiming St. Andrew's business to the entire staff at headquarters when she talked on the phone. He'd call her at home after Compline and invite her to confer with him in his office, or, better still, they could walk together near the lake. He needed to show her the desecration in the crypt, so perhaps the walk would provide a better setting for all his disclosures. And, of course, she should be told about the chute in the sacristy alms door that had been tampered with.

His conscience relieved, the Abbot leaned back in his chair and began to ponder the spiritual chaos that seemed to be swirling throughout the monastery. He thought about Jung's ideas regarding contemporary society, how it hadn't even begun to face its shadow. This certainly seemed to apply to his community presently. Through his study of Jung's views about the human personality, he knew that the more ignorant we are of the shadow, the darker and denser our shadow side is. The undeveloped side of the human personality was seen as composed of all the undersided traits humans deny they possess. And, unfortunately, the composite shadow would become projected onto those in *its* path.

Lately, Fr. Malachi had been fascinated by a process called 3-2-1 initiated by Ken Wilber, philosopher and founder of the Integral Institute, in which individuals attempt to illuminate their shadows and work to integrate those denied parts of themselves. The 3-2-1 practice uses shifts from third- to second- then to first-person. In the third person, the processing individual confronts that which triggers an emotional reaction in him or her, someone who persistently angers him, perhaps. The processing individual faces that person, either in his imagination or actually, and writes a description of him. In the second person, the processing individual talks to the person angering him, writing a dialogue and taking the other person's side as his own. In the third person, the individual *becomes* that person and writes down what the other person has to say about the processing individual's anger. The traits taken on by being that person who angers him will probably be those the individual denies in himself... or his *shadow*.

Fr. Malachi could see that Fr. Jean and Br. Peter would especially benefit from the process. He meditated on its usefulness. Perhaps the 3-2-1 couldn't solve murders, but it could help his monks deal with their shadows so that they could achieve more oneness with the community. On this thought, Fr. Malachi fell asleep in his chair.

◌ဢ

Detective Zelda Wagner didn't usually suffer fools gladly, and she felt considerable surprise when she actually invited Roger Cardiff over for a third visit to her apartment. He was a ruddy-faced man with a shock of reddish gray hair who had no real social graces and appeared to be approaching 70, an age she was prone to declare 'over the hill.' Roger was a rough-neck 'oilfield hand' who had worked with an independent oil company in Iran before the dawn of the Islamic Revolution. His weary blue eyes with deeply etched shadows beneath revealed the evidences of long-term dissipation, and Detective Wagner knew he was a heavy-drinking womanizer who worked abroad most of the year so he could escape the obligations of married life and return stateside for a few months of R & R each summer. He had been separated from his wife so many years, he hardly remembered what she looked like. She was just a wispy apparition materializing in a demanding voice that periodically asked for large sums of money, Roger had confessed to Zelda. He had lived this way for forty years. Roger was interesting to her only because he *could* be entertaining. He loved to dance, dress up in formal attire, and impress waitresses with his bad manners and generous tips in fine dining restaurants, particularly those where New Orleans or Creole cuisine was served. Yet he was ultimately uninteresting to her, except for in the one place that mattered — bed. Detective Wagner knew she was a ruthless woman, but she reasoned that if she hadn't been ruthless before she entered the police academy, she would have become so after a few years of dealing with the underbelly of Marksville.

When Fr. Malachi's call came, Detective Wagner had finished the preliminaries of dinner out with Roger, and they were drinking coffee laced with Tia Maria. Roger had removed her blouse and had begun unzipping her green leather skirt. She was experiencing this warm tingle in the center of her body when the telephone rang. Roger watched her face register irritation and smiled.

"Detective Wagner," she answered the call impatiently.

"Fr. Malachi here."

Detective Wagner slipped out of her skirt and let it slide to the floor. "Yes? Please don't tell me you've discovered another body."

Fr. Malachi cleared his throat. "Thank God, no. However, I've come upon a few pieces of possible evidence, and we need to talk."

"Now?" Detective Wagner raised her finely penciled eyebrows and gazed cynically at Roger, who stood before her in the buff, except for his black socks. He sipped the coffee and liqueur, staring invitingly at her while his left hand curled around her free hand and stroked her palm with a feathery motion.

"No, no," the Abbot protested. "In the morning, after early Mass. Can you meet me at the lake? I don't think any of this collection will disappear in the night."

"I certainly hope not, or I might suspect you of tampering with evidence."

"Indeed! Well, good night, then."

Detective Wagner replaced the receiver, grasped Roger's hand, and led him into the bedroom. "The ever-present Abbot. He just thought he'd save me from a night of irresponsible physical pleasure," she said, clicking off the bedside lamp and succumbing to the hands of her silent, rough-neck lover, this man who made her life almost bearable.

∞

Fr. Malachi hadn't invited Detective Bronson to the meeting she had scheduled with Detective Wagner, but she decided to take her assistant along because he possessed a sharp sixth sense for ferreting out clues. They drove up to the monastery early and sat, silently watching the sun break through the mist shrouding the lake.

Detective Wagner had been up too late the night before and felt no compunction to talk. She was tired... tired of Fr. Malachi's protestations about his flock's innocence and, after the night's romp with Roger Cardiff, she was physically tired. She hoped that this meeting wasn't another wild goose chase, and she had no real hopes that it would provide resolution of the case. Roger Cardiff could be disposed of easily enough because a womanizer was always eager to move on. Actually, she was very lonely and despite her instincts for surviving an affair with a married man, and though she was reluctant to admit it even to herself, she cared about Roger. She realized that she was guilty of self-deception. Her promiscuity was only a screen that hid the truth: she was afraid to enter another committed relationship. Detective Wagner sighed deeply.

"Well, they should be coming out of Mass shortly," she told Detective Bronson.

"Wonder what the old bird has under his stole this time," Detective Bronson said. He was unshaven and bleary eyed.

Detective Wagner thought she smelled alcohol, the odor that comes through the pores of the skin after an all-night drinking bout. "Have you been drinking?" she snapped.

"Not this morning. Just a bit of bar hopping on the Square last night. I'm good for the day. Hopefully, we can knock off early."

Detective Wagner shrugged and got out of the police car. Remembering the debauchery of her own night, she chided herself for asking him anything.

Fr. Malachi emerged from the chapel. "Good morning," he said, smiling tentatively. "I thought perhaps you'd like to take the air, as the Cajuns say, while we talk about some new developments."

119

"I hope they're not blind alleys," Detective Wagner said. "We're anxious to make an arrest."

"Not likely to make one here," Fr. Malachi protested.

"You do stretch this good shepherd role a bit," Detective Wagner said. "Surely your experience of human nature has informed you that even the Religious are capable of killing?"

Fr. Malachi walked on, slightly ahead of the two detectives, controlling his annoyance at the repeated remarks of the harsh female who insisted on implicating his monks. By the time they reached the cemetery, he had become calmer, and he gestured to them to follow him into the fenced yard around the crypt. He opened the vault and lit a candle from the ledge inside the door before the detectives entered.

"This is part of what I found yesterday," he explained. He raised the candle to illuminate the coffin so they could view the dried blood smeared across its top. "I also found a clay doll, a black candle, and a holy card, all of which are now in my office... and, oh yes, a bone that may be a human bone."

"Voodoo again," Detective Bronson said quickly. "Probably a bone from the coffin itself." He took the candle from Fr. Malachi and looked more closely at the coffin lid. "It has been opened. And the bone you've found probably came from the body inside. Who's buried here?"

Fr. Malchi hesitated. "An old monk who came to us from St. John years ago," he said. "He was a transfer."

Fr. Bronson looked questioningly at the Abbot for a few seconds. "And..."

"And nothing more," Fr. Malachi replied quickly.

Detective Bronson continued to stare at the Abbot, then handed the candle to him and abruptly stopped questioning him. He left the crypt and began searching the yard.

Meanwhile Detective Wagner had discovered the extension ladder. "Is this always here?" she asked.

"No, I'm afraid that it may have been used to do more mischief," he said. "It occurred to me that it could've been used to climb up and deface the angel on the ceiling of the chapel."

Detective Wagner, now fully awake, frowned at the Abbot. "You didn't mention this fact in the interrogation," she snapped. "The plot is thickening. Is this a ladder that belongs to the monastery?"

"I had never seen it before yesterday."

"Couldn't it have been in the farm shed?"

"I know every piece of equipment on this property."

"Well, obviously not, since all of these objects that have appeared are unknown to you."

"They're recent additions to our inventory," the Abbot said wryly.

Detective Bronson appeared in the door of the crypt. "I need to see the bone," he said. "I think it may have been used for conjuring. Usually the person who digs up a human bone thinks the spirit of the dead person is contained within the bone and will provide some kind of help from the 'other side' to the conjurer. He uses the bone in a ceremony; thus, the black candle and the doll. The doll was probably meant to be an effigy of the person who was to become the victim of an evil act. I need to see all of your findings."

Fr. Malachi nodded. "But before we go to my office, I have another bit of tampering to show you," he said resignedly. He thought to himself that he might as well come clean about the ashes, the ceiling, the chute in the sacristy alms door—should make the full confession of evidence found. So far, these discoveries hadn't led him anywhere, and he doubted that the detectives would do any better at solving the murders from the clues provided. To him, the most apparent activity going on at his monastery was voodoo, and a voodooiene was behind the murders. All the *hows* and *where* was the *who*? He led the detectives toward the chapel, feeling decidedly feckless.

෬

John Landry, returning home from The Camellia Bar and an evening of hard drinking and failed attempts at seducing a partner for the night, saw the conflagration before he crossed the bridge leading to Mill Pond Subdivision. He was horrified to see the awful red and yellow flames illuminating the night sky. He drove across the bridge and entered his neighborhood. People huddled in the middle of his street in the posh subdivision, watching firefighters aim streams of water from coils of fat hose at a California-style stucco and batten mansion. My god, it was his home! Landry's heart skipped a beat, and he felt cold perspiration appear on his forehead. He braked his car, and putting his head down on the steering wheel, sobbed aloud. Then he lifted his head and looked toward the scorching inferno, now turning his dream home to ashes, along with his precious antique furniture, paintings, the grand Aubusson and Persian silk rugs, his papers—everything—including the list he had stolen from Fr. Paul's room, he thought ruefully. If he had been a religious man, John Landry would have concluded that God's retribution was ablaze on his lawn. He knew that someone like Jerry Falwell or Pat Robertson would have declared that God was venting His wrath on him because he was not only a gay man, he was a greedy man.

Landry thrust the ludicrous thought away and got out of his car to face the heartbreaking desolation. He had lost all. No future CD sales could replace the furnishings, the paintings he had inherited and collected over a lifetime. He felt tears wetting his cheeks and attempted to control himself before pushing through the crowd being held back by several firefighters.

"What happened?" he asked a person he assumed was a neighbor. Landry actually knew no one in the neighborhood.

"Jones," the neighbor said, pointing to the house in front of them, "Jones saw a person—a boy or a very small man—in the neighborhood earlier. He was carrying a can of something. It was gasoline, I reckon. Jones thought that someone had run out of gas, and this person was carrying enough to funnel into a gas tank to start a car. He said the man had large ears and looked sort'a strange, retarded like. That part would make sense. One of the firefighters investigating the fire told Jones that the majority of arsonists have a low I. Q., maybe as low as 70, but they're also mighty angry at something. Most of them were abused when they were kids."

The neighbor regarded Landry curiously as he conveyed this information loquaciously, not unlike a newscaster feasting on sensationalism, Landry thought. He shivered, and feeling his stomach turn, walked on toward his enkindled home. Sparks flew through the air, and the roar of crackling flames pierced his ears. The noise of glass shattering told him that the windows of his mansion had begun to blow out. The most heartbreaking sound was that of the old cypress beams in the mansion's ceilings crashing loudly. His brain reeled, and he felt as though it had been invaded with and filled by the whitish smoke drifting in the oppressive air.

A firefighter, swathed in black squad suit and helmet, held up a restraining hand as Landry moved closer to his own ruined house.

"No further or you'll be in the heat zone," the firefighter said.

"I'm the owner," Landry said bitterly, falling into the firefighter's arms and quickly succumbing to one of his 'faint heart' swoons.

# CRAPTER XVII

*We believe that the divine presence is everywhere and that in every place the eyes of the Lord are watching the good and the wicked... Let us consider, then, how we ought to behave in the presence of God and his angels, and let us stand to sing the psalms in such a way that our minds are in harmony with our voices.*

≈ **From the Rule of St. Benedict**

The weeks following the tragic loss of the two monks at St. Andrew's were spent in *practice* of chant, in both senses of the word, Fr. Malachi stressed, as he admonished his monks on the Saturday before Christmas. Continuing to sweetly fill the air with this 'harmony of angels' *was their monastic* vocation, their *spiritual practice*, each line of the choir's blended sound embodying its own light and energy in the familiar phrases of the psalms and the responses.

Fr. Jean had reluctantly become their lead voice, their cantor *and* choirmaster, replacing Fr. Paul; and the monks knew they were in a new phase of outreach. Interest in the monks at St. Andrew's and their ground-breaking first album had led to a fever-pitch demand for a sequel. The demand was especially driven by the intriguing shadow under which they now lived daily.

The second kind of *practice* for the production of the new album, *Godspeak II*, to be recorded the week after Christmas, was the goal that kept the monks from completely losing their equilibrium and questioning their purpose. It was clear to them and to their Abbot that it was their duty to let their voices shine forth with the light of Christ. The voices were to be tangible witnesses that *not even death* could silence this work of the soul that their ancient tradition continued to offer in a world grown deaf and blind to the Spirit's movement among all peoples.

Of course, they hadn't yet fully faced the problem that there would BE no more innovative chant variations now that Fr. Paul, their composer, was no longer there to play around creatively with the sequences of the tones.

Fr. Malachi's lofty thoughts came to an abrupt halt when he was summoned to his office for a phone call. "Carry on," he motioned to Fr. Jean, whose dark eyes betrayed the uneasiness he still felt in this starring role in The Heavenly Choir. However, Fr. Malachi believed that his Prior had the spiritual depth and commitment to bring them all through this crisis.

Despite the police and lab work that had gone on in the last two-and-a-half weeks, the case of the murdered monks was far from solved. Detective Wagner had ascertained that the rubbery white and gray fragments found around the altar after Fr. Paul's murder had been crumbling pieces from deteriorating rubber soles, shards scuffed off of cheap running shoes. Since all the monks had pairs of such shoes from the same supplier, it hadn't taken long to determine that none of them matched the forensic samples collected. But Detective Wagner had been able, in her caustic style, to complain loudly about not "finding a frickin' monastic Cinderella that this shoe fits!"

Even she had recently grudgingly admitted that none of St. Andrew's monks, all so meticulously interviewed by her and her team, were suspects in the grim murders. However, a slight cloud still hung over Fr. Jean because of his Haitian understanding and cultural tolerance of voodoo, and the shrewdly perceptive woman detective had picked up on the former rivalry between Fr. Jean and Fr. Paul (even though Fr. Malachi had kept hidden the note that would have shown Fr. Paul's intent to meet his rival in the chapel that night). Although Fr. Malachi had seen Fr. Jean go to his room and close the door after their late-night walk on that fateful night, no one could vouchsafe that he hadn't later returned to the chapel to meet with Fr. Paul. Fr. Malachi simply knew that he had not.

As for Fr. Eli, Detective Wagner had found everything about him and his peripatetic presence in the Abbey baffling. But then, so had everyone else. A more complete study of his manuscript had turned up no indication that physical violence was in his plan. Nor was his anger particularly directed against Fr. Paul, even though the former cantor had introduced the altered chant and, to Fr. Eli's mind, knocked the Abbey off course in its revered traditions and purpose, just as Fr. Eli's own sharp sword had knocked Fr. Paul out of position forever.

Apparently, as Fr. Eli's writings progressed, it had become evident that he himself expected to be 'air-lifted' out of the whole situation, much as the Old Testament prophet Elijah himself had been "taken to heaven in a chariot of fire." That revelation left their sacred stories wide open to Detective Wagner's sarcastic comment that the old prophet had been 'expecting to join up with the Mother Ship in the near future.'

Fr. Malachi knew even more. Fr. Eli had once confided to him that he had terminal cancer and did not expect to live out the year. The old man's own transfiguration had come to him earlier than that, on the shore of their tranquil lake. The police had determined that he had indeed slipped, but someone had finished him off by using a rock nearby to strike him on the head. If the police could find whose soles had shed rubber fragments in the chapel, perhaps they'd also find the hands that had wielded that rock.

Meanwhile, *Come, Lord Jesus...* It was still Advent, after all, and they'd go on, liturgically, fully, *down into the darkness,* anticipating the Light of Christ to be lit, at their Christmas Eve vigil, for another more hopeful year.

Chant would lead the way.

Fr. Malachi felt that a certain profanation, or loss of holiness, had pervaded his domain, and the disintegration of unity had threatened his own centeredness. Just yesterday, as he approached his office, he had glimpsed Cotille crouched behind his desk, placing a strange object in his bookcase. And when she turned to find him observing her, she had muttered something about "all the dust on your books." She had scurried out, and he had searched the shelves and discovered an effigy behind one of his commentaries. Voodoo again! Profanation again! He had left his office and sought out Cotille where she was planted in front of the library, dusting the entry door.

"Cotille, I want you to set aside some time in the morning after breakfast to meet with me."

"What about?" she asked sulkily.

"About this," he said, holding up the crudely made doll.

Cotille seemed unperturbed by the confrontation, and her face remained as impassive as ever. "I can't be long talking."

You're never long talking, the Abbot thought. "We'll talk as long as it takes to explain this object," he said, shaking the doll at her.

Cotille stepped back and gave him a malevolent look. She nodded assent and lowered her head, folding her waxing cloth carefully into a neat square.

◯R

Now the hour had come for her to meet with him, and he waited impatiently for her to show up. He had time to recite three Hail Mary's before she appeared in the doorway, dressed in a clean blue denim jumper and yellowing white blouse.

"Good morning, Cotille," the Abbot began graciously.

"I can't be long talking," she said, repeating her protest of the day before.

"And I'll determine that," Fr. Malachi said emphatically. "Why did you put this effigy in my office?"

"It was to uncross me."

"Cotille, I don't know much about voodoo, but I do know that effigies are used to cross, not to uncross."

She smirked at him. "Sometimes voodoo makes a blessing."

"We have rituals for blessings here, and you know it. Why should I need this doll to bless me?"

"Well, sometimes a doll can stop a person from interfering with what another person wants to do — like stop someone from gossiping or telling secrets."

"And what secrets would I be telling that you felt warranted this doll's intervention?"

"I don't know about that word 'inter-vation,' but maybe you let out the secrets I told you about that priest trying to do bad things with me when I was five years old."

"Cotille, I don't violate the rules binding personal confessions."

She stared at him, skepticism heavy in her face. "All the priests look at me like they know, and I hear them talking about me not going to Confession."

"My dear child, you're misguided. What could I possibly gain from broadcasting your confession? We are bound, also, to follow our Rule. 'I have put a guard on my mouth. I was silent and was humbled.' I forbid vulgarity and gossip here and refrain from it myself."

Cotille lowered her head. "Your wife hated you," she said suddenly.

The Abbot was startled at the outburst. "What?"

"She hated you and asked me to poison you. She promised me that *ring* on your finger if I'd do it." She glanced at the bulky gold ring with the ancient Jesus coin on his right hand, worth many thousands of dollars. It was actually priceless. "She even bought the arsenic and told me how to put it in your drink before supper. I was afraid to do it, and she got mad at me. You're lucky to be alive."

Fr. Malachi put his face in his hands. He wanted to cover his ears, but he had invited the conversation, and the truth was in his face. In her last months, Virginia had turned on him, as those who are mentally disturbed often do, succumbing to violent rages, even spitting at him. But he had been patient, thinking it was symptomatic of bipolar disease. He couldn't believe that she had actually deteriorated to the point of wanting to kill him!

A dense silence filled the room, and he lifted his head to look at the disturbed woman sitting before him. Her shoulders drooped, and she refused to meet his eyes. A phrase from Jung flickered in his mind: "The destruction of the God image is followed by the annulment of the human personality..." Here was someone clinging to symbols of voodoo, a religion from which authentic life had departed. Here was something deadly, although Cotille had confessed to having refused to use the lethal substance when she had the opportunity. As shaky as he felt from hearing the terrible truth about Virginia, he had to offer this woman absolution.

"So what do you really hope to accomplish with your voodoo activity?" he asked.

"I want to attract the protection of spirits," Cotille answered. "Someone has crossed me."

"How do you know that you've been crossed?"

"I feel bad, sick. Very sad. And I'm afraid that bad spirits and many demons are in my house and after me. Someone wants to do me harm." Cotille's black eyes finally met Fr. Malachi's, almost beseechingly.

"So you wish to do harm to people around you to get rid of that feeling? You obviously seek influence over your environment.

Why don't you invoke the Divinity, pray to God, ask for grace and harmony in your life? You're in a perfect place to do that," Fr. Malachi said gently.

Cotille smirked. "You think your monks would help me?" she scoffed. "They use their prayers to strike fear in people's hearts—all their talk of hell and sin."

"Cotille, have you ever considered that you hate them because you're afraid of them? I think the monks have been kind to you."

"They don't even see me."

"So have you ever heard of the law of radiation and attraction? It means that you attract people with good energy, particularly if you wish to help them. You appear to want just the opposite of that in your daily life here."

Cotille shrugged and lowered her eyes again.

Fr. Malachi sighed. She is either ignorant or obdurate, he thought, but the least I can do is absolve her. "Cotille, your fears will disappear if you promise to express contrition and receive absolution from me."

Before he could explain further, she snapped, "O.K., I'm sorry then." Cotille crossed herself and folded her arms across her breast in a contradictory motion of resignation and defiance.

Fr. Malachi sighed and pronounced the absolution carefully, feeling that she had at least made a stab at confession and contrition. *"Passio Domini nostril Jesu Christi, merita Beatae Mariae Virginis..."*

As Fr. Malachi intoned the prayer of absolution, he wondered if he was committing sacrilege. Perhaps Cotille would be helped, but he must exact some kind of promise from her that she would stop practicing black magic on the grounds of the monastery.

Before he could assign a penance for her, she exploded again. "Fr. Jean believes in voodoo too. He met with me about how to get uncrossed, and instructed me. He's not the saint you think he is."

There's no real penitence here, Fr. Malachi thought. She makes one accusation after another. "I know about that meeting, Cotille."

"You don't know what he told me. He's another snake priest wearing a mask. He was jealous of Fr. Paul. He probably killed him. He knew how to *cross*, how to make the evil eye and put *gris-gris* on people. He believes in voodooienes." Having made a confession, a half-hearted act of contrition, received absolution, and then rebounded to malicious accusations, Cotille left the office before she could be given a penance to perform.

Fr. Malachi doubted that she would have enacted one anyway. She was lost, and he hadn't done anything except push her further back into the hell of her life, the gates of paradise clanging shut behind her. She had rejected the chance for movement in her spiritual life with impunity. Cotille was more distant from her Divine source than he had imagined. He must find Jean and question him. It was just like Cotille and her crippled mind to incite doubts in him about his Prior. "What a vipers' tangle," he said aloud. He felt a tremor of fear when he left the office and began saying the Jesus Prayer as he climbed the stairs to Jean's room. Cotille's fixation had undone him as surely as Marie Lauveau had undone so many people, with the snakes she used to inspire herself to speak with the lips of evil spirits. He so needed Jean's reassurance.

&#x0298;&#x0280;

Fr. Jean was at his desk, staring out the window at the preening geese beside the lake, a sheaf of music manuscript sheets spread out before him, when he heard the Abbot's rap on the door. He turned in his chair and motioned for his superior to enter.

"I'm sorry to take you from your work on the Chant," the Abbot said. "I seem to have stirred up a hornet's nest with Cotille and need to counsel with you."

A look of repulsion flickered across Fr. Jean's face. "What's she up to now?"

"She's obsessed with voodoo and making a strong allegation about your involvement. I just wanted some reassurance that you aren't dabbling..." the Abbot said tentatively. He wasn't prepared for the outburst of his Prior.

"Damnit, I've told that woman, and I've told you that I don't mess with primitive black magic. Seems like you must be succumbing to something yourself—doubting me like this. Do you really think I'd get involved in these vassal tribe rituals and fetishes?"

"I'm sorry," the Abbot said quickly. "Cotille's behavior just unsettled me momentarily."

"Well, if you think that I'm doing conjuring work around here, perhaps I'd better resign as your Prior," Fr. Jean said stiffly. "Do you want to summon the brothers to counsel?"

"Jean, Jean, there's no need for us to exaggerate the problem. I couldn't run this monastery or direct the choir by myself. You know you're indispensable. Please forgive the question and, at the same time, I admonish you to watch your temper. This reaction is so unlike you."

Fr. Jean stood abruptly and held out his hand to the Abbot. "I'm sorry too. All of us have become so suspicious of one another. We seem to be suffering from collective doubt and have begun to put God beyond our lives, rather than recognizing that He is working within us. I guess it's the fact of unsolved murder in our midst that has caused such prolonged tension. I know I've felt some estrangement lately from my brothers and from God."

"Well, we've allowed the doubt to seep in and alienate us from each other," Fr. Malachi said. He embraced his Prior and sat down before his desk. "What do you think Cotille is really up to?"

"My question precisely," Fr. Jean said. "Do you think she's somehow connected to the killings?"

"Oh no! I think she has a warped mind, but I don't believe she's capable of murder." The Abbot remembered Cotille's confession of her inability to poison him. "She has an enormous store of ill will toward the Brothers, which makes me wonder why I gave her this job after Virginia died. But I don't think she's a murderer. She seems to be deeply confused about something. She did prove to be a wonderful caretaker for Virginia, in those last months, and I guess my sentimental reasons for keeping her employed here have caused me to be less harsh in my judgments of her. The police have interviewed Cotille, have even forced her to give up those disintegrating shoes she shuffles around in, to see if the pieces of rubber found around the altar match that of the soles. But Detective Wagner says there wasn't a match, and she doesn't regard Cotille as a suspect. Cotille, after all, has an airtight alibi for the night of the murder. She was sedated and detained in the infirmary for the night after being treated for her burned hand that evening. I think the police around here encounter voodoo practitioners all the time," he added. "I know Cotille's activities are bizarre, but as a murderer she isn't on my radar, as the young folks say."

Fr. Jean shrugged his shoulders at the long explanation. "I'm not so sure she wouldn't commit murder," Fr. Jean said. "If a person really believes in the power of voodoo, sometimes the psyche is deeply affected, the Shadow becomes more dense, and he or she becomes capable of anything."

The ominous sentence hung in the air of Fr. Jean's room as if poised for a call to attack, and both monks looked at one another in perplexity. The Noonday Prayer bell broke the heavy silence in the room and put an end to their ruminations over the strange maid who lingered in the monastery halls daily.

℞

Fr. Malachi spent the afternoon sleuthing in the infirmary, talking to the meticulous Br. William about Cotille's overnight stay there the night of the murder. Br. William informed the Abbot that Cotille had protested she didn't want to spend the night at the facility and seemed unusually restive while he treated her, afterward going to the window several times as if looking for someone to show up. The young monk had given her a mild sedative and checked on her several times during the night, each time finding her in a deep sleep.

Fr. Malachi wondered why he felt so relieved when he found that Cotille had been too sedated to have slipped out and murdered anyone. Maybe he needed to practice the 3-2-1 exercise he had thought about recommending to Fr. Jean and Peter, he mused. He himself seemed to be carrying a lot of baggage about Virginia, enough to make him protect a woman who had blatantly practiced voodoo on the monastery grounds and who had once briefly considered murdering him!

Now Compline had ended, and here he was, still in his office, contemplating scenarios concerning the monastery murders. He was annoyed that he couldn't pray away the oppressive thoughts he had about the Devil lurking on the premises. His Bishop had laid the cross on his heart and his head, commissioning him to solve the murders and clear the air of anything that would sully the pure voice of Chant, and their reputation as an Order. Now he had become obsessed with the investigation. Each hour that passed, he neglected his prayers and pondered, instead, the intricacies of murder. He had even considered going to the library in town to check out old Agatha Christie mysteries to read, as if the Grand Dame could uncover for him pertinent clues and help him name the killer.

The Abbot glanced out his office window and was startled to see a light flickering near the lake. A black and white police car had been parked at lakeside all day, but he had surmised that Detective Wagner would leave at nightfall, and obviously she hadn't. Or was it someone else? The Abbot went to the window and peered into a very dark night. The light now seemed to be concentrated in one spot, and he strained to see two cars parked by the lake. A police car and a sleek vehicle that could have been a Lincoln or a Cadillac — he couldn't identify the larger car in the darkness — were parked alongside one another.

Fr. Malachi felt his temper rise. He knew the police had skulked about the grounds during the day, but this nighttime activity was a real invasion of monastery privacy. He buttoned his black wool cape at his neck and left the office, quietly closing the door of the administration building and walking toward the lake.

As he approached, he heard the angry voices of a woman and a man arguing. The woman's voice was that of Detective Wagner, and she wasn't sparing any words as she barked at a tall man standing in a pool of light beaming from the headlights of the police car. The man wore a windbreaker and blue jeans, and the expression on his dissipated-looking face was crestfallen as Detective Zelda Wagner shouted at him. "Damnit, I told you that I didn't want a permanent partner who was already married. You've bedded enough floosies to know how to leave a woman. Now, just get lost, Roger. You'll never change. Read my lips, we're caput."

Before the man could protest, Fr. Malachi cleared his throat loudly. Startled, Detective Wagner pulled a semi-automatic revolver from the holder around her waist and clasped both hands around it, pointing the weapon into the darkness. "Who's there? Come out into the light," she demanded.

Fr. Malachi mockingly raised his hands in the air and stepped into the light. "Do you have to haunt this property at night or is this your newest place for a tryst?" he asked sardonically.

"Oh, Fr. Malachi. Sorry. Roger was just leaving, and I'm glad you showed up because I have some interesting news to report."

The tall man zipped up his windbreaker, gave Detective Wagner a pleading look, then turned and got into the limousine-sized green Cadillac.

Detective Wagner watched the long car disappear before she spoke again. "Do you want a report here and now, or shall we go to your office?"

"It's a bit brisk out for me, and mind you I'm very tired, but we can go to my office. I really do have serious objections to your lurking around the monastery after dark."

Detective Wagner ignored his objection, opened the door of the police car, and brought out a black and yellow LED flashlight. She seemed calmer now that the man had departed, and holding the flashlight with one hand, she took the Abbot's arm with the other in an unusual gesture of intimacy as they walked toward the administration building.

In the Abbot's office, she exhaled a long breath, brazenly inched her skirt up almost to her thighs, and removed her boots. She leaned back in the uncushioned chair before Fr. Malachi's desk.

"By all means, get comfortable," the Abbot said drily.

"Look, we may have a break in our case," Detective Wagner began. "The State Mental Institution down the road called me about an escaped mental patient today."

"Indeed. And how does that affect this case?"

"Well, it seems that about a month ago, one of their so-called rehabilitated patients, who had been put in a work/residency program, escaped. The patient lived in an apartment on the grounds and could move about freely on the property when he wasn't working in the kitchen. Seems he decided to walk out in the middle of the night. The social workers have just now decided to inform us, and the Sheriff's staff has also begun looking for him. He's a paranoid schizophrenic and could be dangerous. Have you seen anyone who looks like this man lurking around the monastery?" Detective Wagner pulled a crinkled photograph from the pocket of her green skirt and thrust it across the Abbot's desk.

Fr. Malachi peered at the photograph. The man in it appeared to be of an indeterminate age, somewhere between 50–70 years of age. He had a full, straggly beard, and his forced smile revealed that he had no teeth. A curious light glistened in his dark brown eyes. Fr. Malachi recognized it as the look of madness... and malevolence.

"This guy loves Samurai swords and was actually put in the asylum for brandishing one in a restaurant in Frankville, about 30 miles up the road from here. He has a history of at least 25 years of going in and out of institutions—DePaul's in New Orleans, GreenBrier here in Marksville, Charity Hospital, and the Veterans' Clinic in Alexandria. Name a mental health facility; he's been there. The social workers say he is extremely *cunnai,* but he hasn't killed anyone yet. However, the last few years, he has been collecting knives and showed up at the State asylum with a sack filled with them, including an expensive-looking Samurai sword."

"But that was a month ago. Surely he would've been seen somewhere around here or near New Orleans during that time."

"His sister in Frankville says he's good at executing disappearing acts. He thinks he's a magician, among other things, some of them being that he calls himself by the name of his dog, Toby. The Sheriff said she laughed at him when he suggested someone had murdered her brother and thrown him into Lake Ponchartrain. I think he's hiding somewhere near here during the day and comes out at night, like a vampire. Maybe one of the crypts is his home. And, further, I think he came here and offed two monks with one of his prized knives, just for sport. Maybe he was trying to steal Fr. Eli's sword too. If he can't be found, I'll satisfy the Sheriff and sweep the lake again, for a body, but I think we have the perp who has been murdering monks around here."

Images of the voodoo objects they had found at the crypt flashed through Fr. Malachi's mind. An escaped mental patient was the perp? Why not? He sat back in his chair and sighed. "If only this were true," he said. "I don't mean I hope that the poor demented soul committed murder, but at least the heat would be off of my monks."

Detective Wagner picked up her boots and began to pull them on her small feet. "Well, it's the best lead we've had so far, and I'm going to be staking out men on the monastery property for some days to come, so get used to our nighttime presence," she said sharply. "We'll be a fact of life around here for awhile." She gave the Abbot a brief smile and marched out of his office with a case closed look on her face.

The Abbot went around his desk, knelt at the *prie dieu* before the wall crucifix, and began his nightly prayers with "Lord, thank you for giving us a real suspect."

# CHAPTER XVIII

*The ultimate experience of forgiveness brings a change of heart, a metanoia of the spirit, after which every seeming injury, injustice, rejection, past, present or future, every so-called blow of fate, becomes, as it were, an essential note in the music of God, however discordant it may sound to our superficial hearing.*

—Helen M. Luke

Following the burning of his mansion, John Landry had been shocked when Fr. Malachi sought him out in The Camellia Bar to extend an invitation for him to stay at the Abbey as long as he wished. "Until you fully recover," the Abbot had said. "You've done a great service for us by helping us raise money for our work in Haiti... and other projects," he said cryptically.

John Landry had felt like weeping when he accepted the invitation. Dressed in his expensive gray wool suit and an outrageous yellow tie, he followed the Abbot back to the monastery where the two novices, Sean and Peter, welcomed him. They led him to one of the sparsely furnished rooms in the lower hall of the monks' quarters, where he collapsed on the bed and slept for a full day and night.

Landry had been living there long enough, and had been through enough to realize that the ascetic surroundings and Benedictine discipline actually suited him much more than the profligate life he had been living. He had also grown closer to understanding Chant, and had developed a real appreciation for its ancient roots. His new identification with it was at a deeper level than he had had for its contemporary adaptations.

Sean, gifted with gentleness, had shown unusual interest in the publicist and introduced him to the more in-depth spirituality of Christian friendship. John Landry had been, in his words, "softened up." He had begun to probe his need for intimacy and found that the more disclosures he made to his two friends, the more they accepted him. He was learning how to relate, he told one of his gay friends, and had been incensed by the friend's cynical laughter.

When Landry had become calm enough to appreciate the quiet regimen of the monastery, Peter and Sean gave him a book entitled *The Mirror of Love*, by Aelred, of course. And Landry fell in love with his writings. He reveled in the passage that Sean read aloud to him one day when they were seated on the bench beside the trellised walkway. "And this love was free of fear, did not feel offense, hold suspicion, or give any flattery... between us there was nothing fake or phony."

In a further reading, in which Aelred had borrowed from Cicero, Landry became intrigued with the idea that friendship was "agreement on all things sacred and profane, accompanied by good will and love..." Landry sometimes scoffed at his new idea of manly love; but he also pondered the idea of a love that involved purity of intention and permanence. Good Lord, he thought to himself, am I actually considering intentional celibacy? He had no answer as yet.

Meanwhile, *The St. Helena Times* carried a story every day about the still-unsolved murders at the monastery, and the notoriety of the place seemed to spur ever burgeoning sales of the Chant CD. John Landry knew some kind of transformation was taking place in himself when he felt delight that the monastery would have an abundance of money to send to the orphanage in Haiti.

He hadn't returned to his ruined mansion, and the fire was still under investigation by the insurance company. One morning at early Mass, John Landry admitted to himself that he simply didn't care if he owned luxurious trappings anymore. He was happier than he had ever been, living the austere and examined life. He respectfully redoubled his publicity efforts for the CD, and sales of *Godspeak* soared again.

☙

A week before Christmas, the Rt. Rev. James Gregory visited St. Andrew's. He was almost gleeful when he entered the Abbot's office and greeted him by bussing both of his cheeks.

Uh-oh, the Abbot thought. "Your Grace," he said politely.

"Malachi, dear brother. I know you have been enduring

considerable embarrassment with all the adverse publicity lately, but haven't we all? I also see that the sales of our CD, *Godspeak*, have risen rapidly."

"That part of your commission to me is being satisfied," the Abbot said. "However, I'm distressed to report that we haven't solved the murder. We do know of a suspect who, unfortunately, hasn't been found yet."

Bishop Gregory ignored the apology. "I'm sure you'll find the culprit soon enough," he said, oozing cordiality.

"I won't rest until..."

The Bishop interrupted. "The Courts are pressing me, and I feel secure in the knowledge that you'll deliver a check for half the proceeds so we can settle these unfortunate molestation suits," he said. "Perhaps this week?"

"We can supply the money," the Abbot said, "but our agreement is to keep this transaction secret."

"Of course, of course. I'm very glad things are working out for the Abbey. You *will* fulfill the agreement to provide half the proceeds for the Diocese," he said peremptorily. "And now, I must be on my way. I'm due to make a TV appearance for the adoring public about the success of our CD." The Bishop whisked out, filled with self-importance, seemingly unperturbed by the fact that the monks were yet vulnerable to an uncaught murderer.

The Abbot shook his head and assumed his kneeling position at the *prie dieu*. "Good Lord, deliver me from such arrogance," he prayed. "No wonder your Church is in hot water." He refrained from confiding to the Divine what he really felt: He wished that His Grace would get a good scald in the pool of hot water he was causing to swirl about the Church daily. He said a prayer of contrition and left his office, almost stumbling over Cotille on her knees in the hall. Judging from the angry look she gave him, it was clear she had heard the entire conference he had held with the Bishop.

০৪

Detective Wagner met him in the hall. "Another wild goose chase," she said harshly.

Fr. Malachi led her out of the building where Cotille lingered.

"Let's walk by the lake," he suggested. "I can't get enough of the outdoors lately. The place where I feel most at peace is near the lakeshore or in the vegetable garden."

"I'm sorry about your discomfort," Detective Wagner said flatly. "I just wanted you to know that we can't stop searching. I had my assistant, Detective Bronson, check the bank where this mental patient has his SSI check sent, and we found withdrawals, dating back to five days after he escaped. One withdrawal was made in Los Angeles, California, the other in San Diego. After Bronson called several shelters in San Diego, he found the patient had turned up at one facility, and he sent word to his sister, the asylum, and the police that he intended to live there. The State asylum reports that he can no longer return to the rehab program he was in. They only wanted to make sure he wasn't a victim of foul play."

The Abbot's heart sank. They were back at Square One again. And the onus of responsibility to find a murderer was back on his shoulders. He excused himself, waved a hand in the air, and trekked back to his office to pray.

Detective Wagner shrugged at his rudeness and continued to walk around the lake as if she were searching for more clues.

**CR**

Fr. Malachi believed that humans were, in essence, indestructibly valuable, and that the exercise of their will could distance them from, or bring them closer to, the Divine being. He thought it would be simplistic to discount the necessity of privations and upheavals in this life in order to experience the depth of spiritual life, *but he did so revere peace!* His musings brought him back to Fr. Jean's earlier suspicions about Cotille. He was cautious about totally discounting a person's character on the strength of that person's past bad behavior. But now he began to have grave doubts about Cotille's sanity. Her Shadow was dense enough to repel him, but he believed he had some obligation to help her recover her "indestructibly good essence." She appeared to lack an essential humanity that he prayed she must somehow possess. If he was wrong, it meant there was still hell to pay.

Fr. Malachi knew that he often dismissed his intuitions in an attempt to practice compassion and avoid judging people on first impressions. But as he again sat in his office, pondering the murders, he experienced a strong nudge to follow the Spirit, even if he divined it darkly. He felt compelled to reenter the chapel, the scene of Fr. Paul's brutal end. He just felt that something was about to happen in that sacred space again. He had resisted the compulsion to remain in the chapel after Compline, feeling that he merely had a need to remain on his knees longer, for prolonged petitionary prayer. In truth, he had been straining at prayers all day, but his prayers had become vapid and repetitive.

He searched his bookshelves for something to read. Jung, Jung, Jung, he thought, I'm obsessed with his ideas about elevating the personal center into the crux of Divine life. But he can't tell me how to solve a murder! A walk might clear his brain of its darkness, he decided.

However, when he stepped outdoors, he felt pulled toward the chapel again, and a strange terror overtook him. He sensed that he was about to encounter something sinister in the sacred space of the chapel, perhaps a repeat murder? He had forgotten his flashlight and stumbled into the bench by the trellised walkway, thumping against it hard.

"Damn," he said aloud. "Who put that on the walkway?" No one had, of course. He was only walking blind, which seemed to be his typical course lately, he chided himself.

He entered the narthex and went up the aisle to the altar. Marbles of perspiration beaded his forehead as he peered into the gloom of the sanctuary where the altar candles glowed, and a few votive candles flickered on both sides of the aisle leading to the altar. He saw shadows everywhere. In the dim light, the life-sized paintings of the Apostles that Vroon had rendered on the side walls loomed larger and appeared more lifelike. Someone is looking for me, he thought. Someone sinister, who does not wish me well, is looking for me. His legs trembled as he willed himself to open the sacristy door. It made a grating noise when it swung open, and a small, wraith-like form leaped out at him, swiping his arm with a keen-bladed knife. He felt warm blood spurt out and stepped aside as the sprite lunged at him again.

Fr. Malachi sprang into action. With his strong arms, one of which now oozed blood through the sleeve of his alb, he grabbed the small form and forced him to the floor, wresting the knife from the figure's oversized hands. He twisted the small man's arms behind him and held him down by sitting atop his frail back. Fr.

Malachi's hulk easily overpowered the intruder, and he swiftly tied the man's hands behind his back with the cincture he had unloosed from the waist of his alb.

The Abbot went to the sacristy closet and removed an old corporal from a drawer of the chest that held altar linens, tore it in half, and applied the improvised tourniquet to his bleeding arm.

"Who are you and what are you doing here?" he asked the man, kneeling on the floor beside him. The man's elfin face was turned toward Fr. Malachi, and he stared impassively at him, refusing to speak. The Abbot stood and decided to seek help. On the one night he needed Detective Wagner to be on patrol, she had chosen to go home earlier in the evening. He suddenly knew that he had intuited death — his own impending demise — as well as caught, red-handed, the sick soul behind the horrific murders at St. Andrew's. The loss of blood made his head spin and he felt nauseated, most of the sick feeling caused by the knowledge that someone had just tried to kill him. And he had no idea why this strange figure had it in for him.

℘

Detective Wagner and Detective Bronson arrived within thirty minutes, following Fr. Malachi's call informing them that he had found the perp. By that time, he had been treated for a surface arm wound at the infirmary, and Br. William had reluctantly allowed him to leave the clinic. Sean, Peter, and John Landry had been commissioned to stand guard over his assailant until the police arrived.

Fr. Malachi returned to the sacristy and stood gazing down at a man with the scrawny physique of a young boy, yet who was clearly a man, one who had the vacant, questioning eyes of the slow-witted. He wasn't surprised when Cotille entered the sacristy from the outside, opening the door to a scene she couldn't have anticipated.

"Claude," she cried, kneeling beside the emaciated-looking man. "Did they hurt you?" She turned her head and glared at Fr. Malachi. "He's not to blame for anything. He does whatever I tell him to do."

"And does that include murder?" Fr. Malachi asked.

"The only one we ever wanted to kill was YOU," Cotille shouted. "You and your secrets! Bringing Fr. Robicheaux here and covering up his sins, burying him in the crypt with the others like he was a holy man. Did you just conveniently forget he made me pregnant with Claude? He not only molested me, he abused his own son and had to be sent away from St. John. Why do you think I agreed to come here? I needed a bone from his tomb to cause his spirit to seek you out and kill you. You could have told the Bishop about us and pressed him to give us a pot of money instead of giving half of all the Chant cash to the Diocese to take care of old men who molest children, like that devil man Robicheaux. You deserve to die!" Cotille flung herself at the Abbot and reached for his face with her long, dirty fingernails, but Peter pulled her off and held her flailing arms.

"You can't hold me back forever," she hissed at Fr. Malachi. "All of you are demons, except for poor old Fr. Eli who had to be killed when he found Claude washing the katana in the lake after he killed Fr. Paul by mistake. *You* were supposed to die. *You're* the one who was always praying in the chapel at that hour!" Cotille pointed at the Abbot, and he recoiled as she gathered spittle in her mouth and let it fly toward him. "You and your precious ring!"

"Interesting little drama," Detective Wagner drawled, entering the already-crowded sacristy. "I think I have it all on tape, but you can continue your story if you'd like."

"Bitch," Cotille spat at the detective. "You couldn't solve a crime if your life depended on it. We left so much voodoo evidence around, you should have been able to figure something out."

Fr. Malachi crossed himself. "You must have wanted to get caught," he said. "The guilt was destroying you and your son."

"We only wanted to destroy *you*," she said. "He thought it *was* you! You are tall like Fr. Paul, and he wore those boots too. What did the boy know, with your gray-headed skull shaved, looking like Paul's blond stubble-head in the half-light? That ring should have been mine!" Cotille pointed to the large gold ring on Fr. Malachi's right hand. "Claude only wanted the katana Fr. Eli owned. And he had to drop that and lose it, too! He saw the old prophet dancing around with it in The Camellia Bar on St. Andrew's Day and tried to steal it. Only Eli didn't cater to your self-serving celebrations. Then Eli caught Claude washing his own Samurai sword after he killed Fr. Paul by mistake, and Claude stole his katana after he hit him on the head with a rock. Then Claude panicked and threw it in the lake. The real murder weapon is in one of the crypts, but all of you were so stupid, you didn't bother to look any further than his father's bones."

"Anything you want to add to this story?" Detective Wagner asked, checking the recorder to see if it was working properly. She glanced briefly down at Claude's deteriorating running shoes and felt certain that now a match with the shards of evidence would be made.

"She made me put the ashes on the altar and cut out the angel's face," Claude whined. "I crawled through the offering window. It's me who blacked out the 'money-for-monks' poster. And I made a grand fire in that old Queen's house," he said defiantly, with a crooked grin on his face. "'Cause he was stupid enough to spread his suspicions about me to other ears. 'The small one,' he said..."

"Enough," Fr. Malachi said. "Take them away, please. There's too much evil energy discharging in this room." He turned and went out the side door of the sacristy, shutting it firmly against further intrusions.

# CHAPTER XIX

*An old abbot was fond of saying, "The devil is always the most active on the highest feast days."*
— **Edward Hays**

*Music hath charms to soothe a savage beast, to soften rocks, or bend a knotted oak.*
— **William Congreve**

Christmas Eve day arrived mild and windless, devoid of Louisiana fog, and the mellow voices of The Heavenly Choir carried clearly through the open doors of the chapel down to the lake. Fr. Jean was hitting his stride as cantor, it seemed.

The "Christmas Surprise" that no one in the choir expected had been a hidden folder of Fr. Paul's latest chants, found under a pile of blank composition books in his cluttered room.

Fr. Paul, wrestling with himself or other forces, had apparently been led to create these far more sophisticated, mature renderings, surpassing even the best of his already recorded Chants! When would he have shared them with the others if he had lived? Their new album would soon be recorded and dedicated to his memory, revealing the genius behind his troubled psyche.

And the profits from these new recordings would all be handled by the trust that had been created by Paul's family following his demise, with Fr. Malachi's blessing. The Bishop wouldn't be able to tap into these funds, though it was assumed that much of the new profits would go directly to the Abbey and its ministries. Wait until the Most Reverend got wind of that development! Fr. Malachi's conscience would forever be plagued by the sin that he had committed by paying for an attorney to defend a pedophile.

But if he was approached again by the Bishop, he'd refuse to help the old man, and might even expose him. If his refusal to comply meant he'd have to leave his beloved Order, so be it. He could not again be a part of the Church's denial of sin against children.

Malachi thought briefly of the old prophet, Fr. Eli, to whom he had extended hospitality and shelter, perhaps against sound judgment. All the old man had wanted was to spend his last months completing his *work*, which Fr. Malachi had judged harmless at the time. But he had learned that no human efforts were insignificant in the tapestry of the whole. Fr. Eli's presence had been part of the revealing, but not in ways the old man himself could have imagined. *May he and all the souls of the departed rest in peace...* The Abbot crossed himself against any further losses in the coming year.

The Christmas Eve service tonight would be a high water mark of a new beginning for the Order. No one else need know that some small slips of paper, Paul's note to Jean to meet him that fateful night, would be burned along with the Christmas Eve incense.

Fr. Malachi had taken a lawn chair to the lakeside and now sat, languidly enjoying the modal melodies. There was nothing like the continuation of Chant to help restore peace at St. Andrew's, he thought.

His meditations were interrupted by the appearance of Detective Zelda Wagner, who drove up in her usual flurry of dust and screeching tires. She recognized the Abbot sitting at lakeside and waved her arm at him.

"Coming down," she said.

"Lord, save me from any bad news this Holy day," the Abbot said aloud, but he waved back invitingly.

"I just came to tell you that both Cotille and Claude are being tried next month, and they're going to plead insanity," the detective said when she reached his side. "I'm afraid you may end up having them as neighbors who'll live down the road at the Asylum."

"I doubt that they'll ever be sent anywhere around here," the Abbot said. "There are some permanent facilities in the Northeast for those who kill. I think they're called institutions for the criminally insane."

"I know, I know. It was a bad joke," Detective Wagner said. She stood beside the Abbot's chair, listening to the Chant. She suddenly wondered what it would be like to make a Confession to Fr. Malachi. A deep feeling of longing akin to *Sehnsucht*, a kind of causeless melancholy, assailed her. She brushed it aside, saying to the Abbot, "I think I'll go in and listen to them practice awhile," she said.

"Indeed?"

"Indeed. I appreciate good music, you know."

"I'm impressed," the Abbot said, smiling at the tough-minded detective. "I was thinking Fr. Jean should now compose a chant called *Chant of Death*, based on the burial service. You know, 'In the midst of life we are in death...'"

"Too morbid for me, Father, but it'd be interesting. Life and death are always interesting out here." Detective Wagner touched the Abbot's arm lightly and walked away, humming an aria from *Madame Butterfly* and looking more peaceful than the Abbot had seen her since the awful deaths occurred.

The Abbot sighed, thinking: We are creating our own music while we live, therefore we live for God. Chant will fill our lives as long as we have breath...

He leaned back in his chair and let the sunlight bathe his upturned face. I could compose a sermon about all of this, he thought. It would go something like this: As Eliot said: "We are the music while the music lasts."

There is always free will in how we sing it, but also determination, driven by circumstances, heritage. The mixed interaction of our acts and God's, woven into the dimension of time, serves to make up each person's *chant*.

But for now it was enough to embrace the sweetness of the air and become one with the human tones that filled it.

5841660R0

Made in the USA
Charleston, SC
10 August 2010